Of My Many Years of Youth

Emma McNamara

Dedication

for my dad, Paul—
thank you for reading my eight-year-old attempt at an original short
story, "The Man That Married a Ham," and still believing in my
future as a writer
thank you for your patience, your advice, your time

for my brothers, Grant and Max—
thank you for the bond between us McNamara triplets
thank you, Grant, for walking me to my room after dark when we
were six to assure that no monsters could catch me
thank you, Max, for telling me — "stop your tears, sister!" — after
you fainted when we were fifteen

for my mom, Julie—
thank you for everything
rest in peace

1

16 years of youth

There's a ladybug in my hair. And there's something wrong

with that. I know there is.

My long, light chestnut locks are drenched in fruity chemicals—coconut curl-control mousse, strawberry dry shampoo, tropical heat protectant spray. My hair is a toxic fruit salad.

Oh, that poor ladybug.

The creature crawls on soft, gentle waves I achieve by straightening my frizzy curls every morning before lightly curling them again. It's a tedious practice. Tangled in the twists of my brittle locks, the intruder scurries deeper into the maze. And there's something wrong with that.

I flick the ladybug away. There's something wrong with me today.

I'm in school.

High School.

For two and a half more years. Nothing new.

Right now I'm in math class.

For an hour.

And I am *so* stupid.

I am immensely dumb.

I'm not the sharpest tool in the shed, the brightest bulb in the shack. I'm idiotic, dim-witted, moronic. Doltish. Unintelligent. *Not smart.* Sitting here in 10th-grade trigonometry, I feel like a cat chasing a laser dot, while everyone laughs at how stupid I am.

Oh, how I miss the good old days when math was just figuring out how many apples Billy has if he starts with five and eats two. I miss mindlessly coloring the most basic of shapes while sipping away at a much-adored Capri Sun, and I miss coming home from school and watching cartoons without worries. Most of all, I miss being a carefree, younger version of —

"Jessica!" snaps Mr-Math-Teacher-Whose-Name-Is-Currently-Oblivious-To-Me.

"H-huh?"

I jolt, drop my pencil, and watch it roll across the room. Nobody picks it up.

Mr-Math-Teacher responds with narrowed eyes and a sigh.

"Would you like to explain to the class how to solve question number six?"

No.

No, I most certainly would not. Volunteering to answer a question is bad enough. You have the risk of being wrong, but hey, at least you tried! The class might laugh at you, but the teacher will appreciate your efforts. But answering a question against your will? That's a whole different story.

It all starts with the teacher calling on you because you weren't paying attention. Your peaceful daydream of a world filled with infinite puppies and cute little kittens is abruptly interrupted by a harsh slap of reality. That's embarrassing enough. But then asking you to answer a question you, quite obviously, have no recall of whatsoever? They're signing you up for agonizing embarrassment. And as if asking for an answer isn't bad enough, teachers then have the *audacity* to ask the one person who isn't paying attention to *explain* the answer? They're ruthlessly crushing your one and only hope of some mighty angel saving your dignity by signaling the answer to you; *real mature.* Then they find it necessary to just stand there staring at you until you reply. Now that's just cruel. I'm telling you, some teachers are just pure evil. I have a feeling—

Wait… I'm supposed to be answering now, aren't I? Maybe more like half a minute ago? Yep. I peer around a lifeless classroom filled with tedious, awkward silence.

A ladybug crawls on my desk, but when I blink, it vanishes.

"Um… what number am I answering?"

"Number six, Jessica," says Mr-Math-Teacher, arms crossed.

Number six? Oh, right, the one with all the numbers. *Well, of course they all have a lot of numbers, Jess, you idiotic idiot!*

Darting my eyes around the room, I see that, of course, nearly everyone is staring at me. I chew my hair absentmindedly and grimace at the bitter taste of toxic fruit salad. Oh, that poor ladybug.

Maybe I can do this. It's just a math question. It's just high school.

No big deal.

Relax.

Breathe… breathe… brea—

Hyperventilate.

Breathebreathebreathe…

Breathewheezebreathwheeze…

Relax.

Just Breathe.

"Um… well… you see, if you minus the two from both sides, and add the numbers and… cross out 'c,' you get… *sixteen?*"

Nope, that can't be right. Even if I miraculously guessed the correct number, my explanation is still clearly gibberish.

About 50% of the class erupts in laughter, looking at each other but skillfully avoiding my eyes. Another 30% clearly tries to keep a straight face, but fail miserably, causing the laughing population to rise to a staggering 80%. Then there's the 15% who are just *way* too smart and mature to ever laugh at such foolishness. They stare at their desks and shake their heads with that, "Someone please help me, I'm surrounded by idiots," expression.

And then there's Chloe.

Chloe and I have been best friends ever since neither of us knew what the word "friend" meant, and here in high school, we help each other through the occasional mid-teen-life crisis. She's one of those people whose energy could power the world, but she can be totally down-to-earth when I really need her.

Chloe looks at me with empathetic eyes while hopelessly trying to control the class's laughter.

Having experienced this humiliation on several other occasions, I know the routine.

Stage one, denial: stare at your desk and completely fail to acknowledge your peers surrounding you. Stage two, regret: regret all of the life choices that led you to this awful moment and vow to never, *ever* daydream in class again. And finally, stage three, acceptance: if you can't beat 'em, join 'em. Just stop being awkward, give up your dignity, and laugh with them. Because, "Ha. Ha. Ha. I'm *so* stupid, it's *hilarious*, right?"

After going through these three phases I know too well, the class moves on and Mr-Math-Teacher continues to teach us everything there is to know about the triangle; you know, other than it has three sides and pointy tips.

I block out all noise and information I would otherwise be taking in. And I just think. This could be a possible stage four of the TAYFABYAPA (Teacher Asks You For Answers Because You Aren't Paying Attention) routine. In this stage, your mind runs wild from lack of interest in anything the teacher could possibly say. The intensity of it increases upon hearing words such as "test," "grades," "future," and "important." This is also the most dangerous, because if your teacher catches you failing to pay attention again, the three stages will inevitably repeat themselves, except worse.

Nevertheless, I zone out and let my mind drift far, far away from class.

What if one day you wake up and you're a pineapple? And you can't move, communicate, or do anything about it; you're just a pineapple. That would sure be terrible. Also, if it's socially acceptable to eat a donut for breakfast, why not cake? They're the same thing, only different shapes. And why do people call food with cheese "cheesy," yet that noun-to-adjective rule doesn't apply to most other foods? You don't hear people saying, "Wow, this salad sure is lettuce-y." *It really bothers me. And why—*

"*Jess!*"

Chloe sits in the seat directly across from me. She models a tumble of blond curls that rest on her shoulders and never frizz or require much product, and on both wrists she wears several dangling bracelets that jingle with every movement. Her pale skin bears a scar she acquired after her cat scratched her nose when she was three, and her blemishes are concealed in cakey makeup. We share the rare trait of green eyes.

I tell her she's beautiful. She tells me I'm lying.

She tells me I'm beautiful. I tell her she's lying.

We never let each other drown in self-deprecation. Or details. And that's friendship.

Chloe looks at Mr-Math-Teacher now facing the whiteboard and babbling on about triangles or whatever, then back at me.

"He's about to call on you. Everyone can tell you're not paying attention again," she whispers. "Hurry up and wake up before we have another *TAY-FAB-YA-PA* incident!"

Nodding at her with a thankful smile, I return my long-lost thoughts to class. Mr-Math-Teacher continues to write on the board, then swiftly turns around.

"Jessica, if three squared plus four squared equals c squared, what is the hypotenuse of the triangle?"

Panic fills my thoughts, but determination quickly overrides it. I have to get this right. If not for me, for all of the students out there who have ever fallen victim to teachers whose major life goal is to humiliate them. Not today, Mr-Math-Teacher! At least, not *again* today. Within a few moments, I have an answer.

"That would be five."

"That is correct," he says, looking way more surprised than he should. But of course, he doesn't stop there. This is high school, after all. Nothing new.

"Now, if a triangle has a hypotenuse of 30 and a side length of 18, how would you find the missing measurement?"

My hope plummets. I was doing so well, but here in high school, that never seems to last long.

"Um... well... you see..."

An unsettling number of my classmates laugh and whisper to each other. Chloe gives me a sad smile along with a shrug, and defeat captures me, once again.

"I got nothing," I say, ashamed. Within seconds, the class initiates the same multiple categories of response as my first failure.

"*Seriously*, it's not that funny!" I exclaim, while the laughing population laugh louder, the smart population shake their heads with even more annoyance, and Chloe once again attempts to make the class settle down, looking like a traffic-conductor trying to simultaneously control a dozen lanes of cars.

The commotion lives on for about half a minute, then thankfully, the bell rings, telling me class is finally over. I rush out of the room.

English next. I'm pretty sure I forgot to do last night's homework. This is going to be miserable.

Pacing down my school's chaotic, quickly overflowing hallways, I decide I need a break. A break from the stress, the homework, the embarrassment— a break from high school. Do I want to take a two-week vacation to Hawaii? Nothing would be better. Do I think my parents will buy the tickets? Not a chance. Would I be overjoyed to ditch the rest of the school day, go home, and just sleep? Where can I sign up? But right now, all I need is a break. *Any* break. So despite knowing the bell will ring in a matter of minutes, I make my way through the sea of students and sit on a bench next to a large, half-open window.

The glistening sun shines through from the outside world, filling a small area around the bench with natural light. It's a beautiful day here in California, a perfect day for being outside. It's a perfect day for walking along beaches, a perfect day for just sitting in the warm, yet gentle sun. It's a perfect day for not being stuck in high school.

Maybe if I sit here forever, all of my problems will go away. Maybe, the longer I stay here, the better things will get. Or maybe I'm just delusional. Despite my better judgment, I ignore the persistent little creature of wisdom inside my brain telling me, '*Get up, you dim-witted buffoon!*' And I take a relaxed breath amidst the mighty tornado of stress.

I look up to see Rye. He's my boyfriend.

We've been dating for a year and a half now. I can still remember the first time we had a real conversation, which was after he fell off the monkey bars in kindergarten ten years ago. I've always liked Rye. We've been together through every day of high school, and no matter how stupid I may be, I would never put that at risk.

He stares at me with gentle, honey-brown eyes, his smooth, bronze skin glowing in the sunlight beaming through the window. His 5'11 stance towers over my 5'2, and from the low-set bench beside the window, I feel like a speck of dust in a storm of shaky scenery.

Rye runs his fingers through his short, deep-brown hair and sits next to me.

"Rough morning?"

"You guessed it," I say. "Math class went horribly."

"Again?"

"Unfortunately. I'll never be smart enough to be anything other than an idiotic idiot. "

Rye chuckles, lightening the atmosphere my worries have created. Leaving his gaze for a brief moment, I relish the beauty of the world outside high school. I have a sudden urge to break the window, to shatter the glass until I'm free. But I'm stuck here. Some things I just can't change.

"You'll be okay," he says, wrapping his arm around me. "Try to forget about math. It won't matter later."

I wish it were that simple. But it's more than math that's on my mind. Something else is wrong, but I just can't grasp it.

"I should get to class," he says, standing. I remain still. "Wanna walk with me?"

I shake my head. "I think I'll stay here."

"Are you okay?"

"I'm fine," I say, wishing it were completely true. "Just tired."

Tired of being a teenager.

"You're smart, Jess. Smarter than you think," says Rye. "Give your day a fresh start."

"I'll try."

"I'll see you in Chem," he says, distancing himself from the bench.

"Bye, Rye."

Gazing out the window, my eyes fall upon the kindergarten next door. It's a small building where five and six-year-olds learn whatever the school system finds it necessary five and six-year-olds learn. Sometimes, I feel as though the kindergarten's location was chosen to taunt us high schoolers, to remind us that life isn't so easy anymore. From many of my classes, I can watch as little kids play freely while I'm stuck inside.

Looking at the playground, I see children everywhere jumping rope, playing hopscotch, and frolicking around with no visible purpose. All of them wear the smiles that come with their youth, and I can hear their joyous laughter from where I sit. It's recess. My heart fills with envy.

They're just living on a cloud, those kindergarteners, letting all the rain fall on the *big kids*.

I remember when I was one of them. I too was eager to grow up and finally obtain the label of "big kid." Now the words "recess," "play," and "fun" sound so foreign they seem to bounce off my brain. I can feel the wrinkles growing across my face like mold, my back hunching; or maybe I just miss the simple life.

Those kindergarteners don't have to worry about getting to their next class. Their teachers will tell them when recess is over, give them a juice box, and bring them inside. Those kindergarteners don't have to worry about a hundred tests and quizzes. If they can recite the first three letters of the alphabet, they get a sticker. If not, they still get a sticker, because, *aww, they're so cute!* Those kindergarteners don't have to worry about the English homework they didn't do. Their biggest care in the world is whether or not they get a cookie with lunch. Those kindergarteners have it easy.

"Jessica," says a familiar female voice.

From her *I-am-so-much-smarter-than-you-so-you-should-probably-listen-to-me* tone of voice, I know she was part of the 15%

who were way too smart to laugh at my mistakes. I know who she is without even looking at her.

Aimee is one of those girls with two major life goals: excel at everything, and make sure everyone knows it. Her vocabulary is three times larger than mine will ever be. When she speaks, her words sound as formal as an MLA-format English essay with proper citations, and of course, she never stutters. Aimee sits on the edge of the bench, probably trying to show our fellow schoolmates still walking to class she isn't actually *friends* with someone like me.

"Yeah?" I respond.

"People who use 'yeah' instead of 'yes' are scientifically proven to lack social skills and basic intelligence."

"What do you want?"

"You do realize that English class starts in 3.5 minutes, correct? After which you have history, followed by chemistry, followed by —"

"How do you know my schedule?"

"I know everything," she says, a sliver of a smile forming on her face. "The degree of illogic which you possess as to simply sit down on a bench with a matter of minutes remaining before you are required to be present in class fills me with mental hardship. I find myself utterly dumbfounded to an even larger degree than I was by your display of idiocy in mathematics, an experience I considered practically inconceivable."

If there's one thing I've learned from high school, it's that you have to have a comeback. But when you're trying to persuade the genius of the school that maybe, just *maybe* you're smarter than perceived, it doesn't usually work. It's kind of like a ladybug attempting to fight off an attacking tarantula. But I always try.

"You know, you're sitting on a bench too. Minutes before you are required to be present in class…"

She responds with a blank stare.

"Yeah, whatever. I have plenty of time," I mumble.

"Why do I even try?" She sighs, standing from the bench and walking away promptly.

Sure enough, about three minutes later, the bell rings and the last few hall stragglers scurry off to class. *Oh no*, I'm late. Feeling only slightly concerned, I fiddle with the locket around my neck. My mother gave it to me the day I was born, and I've been wearing it as a good luck charm every day since I started preschool. It's a heart-shaped necklace with blue tulips engraved on the front and the words "forever young" etched in the inside. Whenever I'm sad, nervous, lonely, or just bored, I hold my locket in my palm for comfort. And every day, I open it and make one wish. This wish can vary from wanting world peace to wanting no math homework.

Today, I have one wish, one hope, and one necessity: I wish to be a kid again. Not a "big kid," but a child, just like those kindergarteners. So I open my locket. And I make my most important wish.

Idly, I continue to stare out the window. In the sky, I see the faint glow of a rainbow, but when I blink, it vanishes.

Most of the children are in clusters accompanied by teachers watching their every move, but one little girl catches my eye. She's all alone and moving toward the window, toward me. She has the loveliest smile and wears a neon-pink t-shirt with purple polka-dot pants. Her light chestnut hair is frizzy with curls, and for shoes, she wears bright yellow Crocs. Around her neck is a heart-shaped, silver locket. She skips freely toward me, reaching the building then standing on her tiptoes. The little girl places her face as close to the window as her little legs will allow, her bright green eyes locking with mine. I recognize her right away.

"It's me!" she says.

6 years of youth

There's a ladybug crawling on the yellow time-out chair in the corner of the room. It's the only bug I don't think is scary.

Mrs. Rose is pulling popsicle sticks from a cup and holds pieces of paper in her hand. Each of the kids has their name on a popsicle stick, and when you get called, you have to answer a question. That means it's time to panic. Everyone stares at you, and when you give an answer, if it's not right, the kids make fun of you, and laugh, and tear you apart! It makes me want to cry, but Mrs. Rose always smiles like nothing is wrong.

Today, when Mrs. Rose pulls a name, she shows that person a card with one word, and their job is to say all the letters in order, which is easy-peasy, and then say the word, which normally is just as simple. And if everybody gets it right, we earn an extra five minutes of playtime at the end of the day. It's very intense.

So far, most of us have been picked, and everyone's answered right, which means it will be my turn soon.

"Kayla," says Mrs. Rose, showing her the card.

"F-r-u-i-t. Fruit," she says with a smile.

I knew that! I would have gotten that one easily. That's just one thing I think is unfair about kindergarten; you only get called on the questions you don't know the answers to.

I wait for my name, only to hear:

"Aimee."

She shows Aimee the second-to-last card.

"B-o-x. Box," she says with her perfect little grin. She's the smart one.

"Great job!" says Mrs. Rose.

That was only three letters! I would have gotten it right. But my mom tells me life is unfair.

"Jessica."

My heart pounds fast as she shows me the card. What even *is* this? I've never heard of this word before! Everyone else gets words as easy as "fruit" and "box" and I get *this*? It has, like, a hundred letters! I panic as I realize I'm the last one today. If I don't get this right, there will be no extra five minutes of playtime, and the class of monsters will never let it go! I can already feel everyone staring at me.

"Um... b-e-c-a-u-s-e," I say, my hands shaking. At least I can say the letters without sounding like an idiot.

"Great job! Now, would you like to pronounce it for us?"

No.

No, I don't want to. Why does she always ask that, but when I say no she makes me answer anyways? This is too much pressure. I think all she wants to do is embarrass me.

"Um... beh-cas-ee?"

"Almost, sweetie, try again," she says, still smiling for whatever reason.

"Bec-ay-se?" I ask with a frown.

"This is a tricky one. Why don't you give it one last go?"

But I don't want to. I can't. I won't. And I know how to get out of this. It's quite simple, actually. It works every time.

"*WAHHH!*"

Right away, Mrs. Rose walks toward me and gives me a hug.

"I'm sorry! You're right, that word is too hard. Do you want a sticker?"

I gladly accept. She holds my hand and walks me over to the sticker drawer while everyone else looks at me with wide eyes.

"The word is pronounced, 'because.' You should all be proud of Jessica for trying!"

I knew that! I use that word all the time. Feeling my face turn red, I look around the room for a friendly face. My best friend,

Chloe, gives me a sad smile, but other than that, no one even looks at me.

Laura, the popular one, raises her hand. Next to her is Mindi, the other popular one. The two of them don't match, and I have no idea why they're friends. Laura is in charge, and always makes sure everyone knows it. Mindi is shyer and lets Laura boss her around day after day.

"Will we still get extra playtime?" asks Laura with a puppy-dog pout. "Just because *Jessica* got it wrong doesn't mean we should all get punished."

Her straight blond hair is held in perfect pigtails, and honestly, I've never been more jealous of anything in my whole life. Mindi has curly brown hair like mine, except hers is a lot smoother are prettier. And longer. And better.

"Of course you can," says Mrs. Rose. "But only *because* Jessica tried her best."

I now officially hate that word. And I officially hate kindergarten. Wanting to disappear, I do what I always do when I'm sad, angry, scared, or just upset: I open my locket to make a wish. Around my neck, I wear a heart-shaped, silver locket my mother gave to me. Today, I have one wish, one hope, and one necessity: I wish to be a big kid. I wish to speed time to when I'm not a kindergartener. I want to experience what it's like to be smart, to have independence, and most of all, to not have the limits that come with being six. I belong somewhere different, but I've been stuck where I am. I'm tired of being bossed around, and I'm tired of being talked to like a toddler. I'm tired of being this young.

So I open my locket. And I make my most important wish.

The class lines up by the door for recess. I stand at the very back, several feet away from anyone else. I don't want them to look at me.

Mrs. Rose leads the way, and we all walk out of the classroom, through the quiet, almost empty hallways, and out the building.

Several other classes are already in neat, single-file lines outside. I've always hated recess. There's just too many people in one place. And I barely ever get to see Chloe, because she has an extra class during recess most days. And just my luck, today is one of them. I have no idea why she does this, but I'm glad I don't have to. Anything is better than class in kindergarten.

Recess can go one of two ways for me: first, I could get one of the five swings, which is ideal. The swings are more fun than any of the other activities, and because everybody wants one, I'll always have someone swinging next to me, even if I don't know them. And the best part is, the other kids almost never try to make conversation. So I don't have to talk to anyone, but no one can judge me for being alone. But if I don't get a swing, like most days, I just walk around the playground pretending to have something to do. Sometimes, I even walk toward the other school next door. You know, the one where all the big kids go.

We walk toward the playground so slowly I don't think we'll ever get there. I'm still at the back, which means, as things look right now, I probably won't get one of the swings. But I haven't accepted defeat. So I quickly make my way toward the front of the line, hoping no one will notice, but the kids look at me funny as I move up. I don't care what they think anymore.

Once we're closer to the playground, I bolt toward the swings, sprinting in the hope that today will be the day I finally get a spot. My hand closes around the chain of the end swing, and I sit quickly. But something is wrong. The soft squeak of the swing is the only sound I hear, and none of the other four are taken. Looking behind me, I realize everyone else is back where the line started, just staring at me.

Mrs. Rose walks toward me ever so slowly.

"Jessica, *sweetie*," she says as if she were talking to a toddler. "You have to wait until I blow the whistle to go to the playground. You know that. But don't worry, you're not in trouble. You'll just

19

have to wait for everyone else to go before you go on the playground now."

In other words, I kind of am in trouble. Everyone laughs as I walk back to the group and hide behind the kids. After they're set free to go, I make my way toward the playground.

There are no swings left.

With a frown on my face and a wish on my mind, I walk over to the bright red seesaw next to the monkey bars. I sit on one end and imagine Chloe on the other as we go up and down, laughing with joy. Then someone gets on the other end. It's Aimee. I don't want to talk to her.

"You do realize a seesaw isn't built for one person to use it alone, right?"

"Please, go away," I say, trying to stay calm.

"But you do realize—"

"GO AWAY!"

She runs off, leaving me alone, at peace. But not for long. Peace and quiet never seem to last long here. This is kindergarten, after all. Nothing new.

The two popular girls, Laura and Mindi, approach me.

"Hey, *crybaby*," says Laura.

"That wasn't nice," I say, because it's the only comeback I can think of. Laura laughs and Mindi soon follows, but I can't yell at them. That will only make it worse.

"Hey, Jessica, did you know that your name has the word 'sick' in it? Jes*sica*!" says Laura with an evil smile. "I feel bad for you. Don't you feel bad for her, Mindi?"

Mindi looks at her friend and pauses for a second before following her lead.

"Yeah, I do feel bad for you, Jes*sica*," she says softly, avoiding my eyes.

"That's not how you're supposed to say my name." I try to sound confident, but instead, my voice is quiet and weak. "I go by Jess, you know."

"Jes*sica*! Jes*sica*!"

Since I can't yell or burst into tears, I walk away from them and move toward the middle of the playground, and they take my spot on the seesaw. I climb the ladder to the monkey bars, the second best activity. But right now, I don't want to use the monkey bars. I want to see Rye. Rye Arthur.

I've always liked Rye. He's actually nice to me, and I see him every day because he's in my class. He sometimes tells the other kids to stop when they're mean to me, and one time, he sat next to me voluntarily during learning time. He even says hi to me at least every other day, and asked me how my day was going once. We're obviously soulmates. But we can't be friends, because he's a *boy*. No boys can talk to girls in kindergarten. You have to wait until you're a big kid to do that. At least, that's what Chloe tells me. But today, I'm feeling adventurous. So when I see Rye on the monkey bars, I follow him. As soon as I do so, he looks back at me and *smiles*! I smile back, try to say something, then choke on my words. But I'm too happy to be embarrassed now.

He continues swinging across, then loosens his grip and falls roughly on the ground. I jump down from the monkey bars and offer him my hand.

"Thanks!" he says, looking at me with soft brown eyes and a shy smile.

"No problem! Are you okay?"

"Yeah, I'm fine," he says, even though I can see his knee is bleeding. "By the way, I'm sorry they were being mean to you over there."

He points to the seesaw where Laura and Mindi sit.

"I like your name. You know, some people think 'Rye' is a weird name too. I think it's a type of grass or something. So I know how you feel."

I try to think of a good response, but before I can speak, Mrs. Rose approaches us.

"Oh, poor Rye!" she says in a high-pitched voice. He blushes and looks at the ground. "Come with me, I'll get you a band-aid for your knee, darling."

They turn and walk away, but before they go far, Rye waves at me!

"See you later, Jess!"

"Um... bye!"

And now I'm alone again. After this is social skills, which is a lot worse than recess. But I'm far too happy to be sad. Rye just waved at me! And he smiled, like, *three times!* I'm not going to let anything ruin my mood. So instead of staying around the playground, I'm going to be adventurous.

I look over at the school next door. You know, the one where all the big kids go. The one I'm not supposed to be in for many, many years.

I wonder what life is like for them. I hear they get to do all sorts of cool things, like make their own lunches and go to bed past eight. Those big kids don't have to worry about getting a swing. They don't even have a playground. Those big kids don't have to worry about not being able to pronounce the word "because." I hear they can read whole chapter books. Those big kids don't have to worry about being anti-social in social skills class. Chloe tells me they have fun classes like history, science, and even different languages! Those big kids have it easy.

Looking at the sky, I see a bright, powerful rainbow. The longer I stare at it, the stronger it gets.

Curious, I make my way toward the building next door. It's a lot bigger than the kindergarten, and has a lot more people. Sometimes, I see them come outside, but I can never get close enough to say hello. But today, I want to talk to one of the big kids.

I wander toward a big, half-open window at the side of the building. Through it I can see a girl sitting on a bench. She's very pretty, and strangely, she's all alone. I wonder why no one is talking to her.

As I move closer, I see she wears a white shirt with a flower pattern and blue jeans. She has long, brown hair and light pink, shiny lips, reminding me of a princess. Around her neck, she wears a heart-shaped, silver locket.

She stares at me with wide, green eyes.

I recognize her right away.

"It's me!" I yell to her.

2

<u>16 years of youth</u>

I stare at the little girl on the other side of the window. She has my eyes, my smile, and she wears a locket seemingly identical to the one around my neck. Although it can't be, I know who she is.

She is me.

With a mix of curiosity and confusion, I leave the bench and run down the now quiet and empty hallways. I know this little girl can't be me, because *I'm* me, and I am sixteen. But at the same time, I have no doubt who she is. I know it is true, but I know it can't be.

Eager to interact with my kindergarten self, I bolt across the grass between the neighboring buildings. She peers into the window, then turns around to see me. We lock eyes. Her mouth agape, my legs trembling with a whirlpool of emotions, we just stare at each other. She waves at me with a shy smile, and I wave back timidly, at a loss for words. And through this confusing affirmation that yes, this is somehow happening, I meet my youth for the first time.

Slowly twirling her curly hair with tiny fingers, my younger self stands still and stiff ten feet away from me, her wide green eyes still focused on me. Her beige, lightly freckled skin is so smooth I envy her, and on her left cheek is the coffee-colored, quarter-sized birthmark I cover with concealer every morning. Chloe says it looks like a giraffe.

My younger years step toward me.

"Hi!" she says with the high-pitched voice I haven't heard since I was her.

"Hello," I say, introducing myself to me. "My name is Jessica. Jessica Jule Locke. And you are—"

"Jessica Jule Locke!" she says, jumping with excitement. "You're the future me, aren't you? This is so cool! I'm so pretty! Well, *you're* so pretty! Do I have lots of friends in high school? What time do I go to bed? Can I drive? Am I famous? Am I—"

"Woah! We'll talk about those things later. Right now, let's figure out how *this*—" I point to her, then back at me, "—is possible."

"I know! I know!" she says, waving her hand in the air. "Today I used my locket to make a wish to grow up and be a big kid. And here you are! Well, here *we* are."

"Wait a minute," I say. "I made a wish too. I made a wish to be young, to be like you again. So if me you wished to be young, and you me wished to grow up—"

"Then *you me us I* are going to switch places!" says my younger self. "I can't believe the locket actually worked for once."

"Open your locket," I say, an idea forming.

"But why—"

"Just open it!"

We both open our lockets, and a piece of thin, folded paper falls out. I unfold my paper and read the words it captures.

"you are young and you are old / you are shy and you are bold / you have many different aspects granted to you from your many years of youth / and you are soon to discover the truth / the age-old question is as so: / does life become better, worse, or perhaps constant as our years grow? / to find the answer, and to forever know

which year is which / your six years of youth and your sixteen years of youth will switch"

"Wow," says my six years of youth. "This is *crazy!*"

"Read yours."

She looks at the paper from her locket and shakes her head.

"I can't."

Then, out of nowhere, the message reads itself. The voice is familiar, yet impossible to grasp.

"only at school will you switch your years / this should protect you from at-home tears / communication with your other self during the switch is something that cannot happen a lot / this experience will require your true, independent thought / do not tell others about your youth's tricks / or you will have problems you cannot fix / your shared wish is to be granted to you both / and may only be undone in synchrony to your new oath / you may not forever return, or fix this trick in the slightest / until you decide that of your many years of youth, yours have been the brightest / now switch your lockets, and don't look back / the school day will start over to launch you on the right track"

In unison, we place our pieces of paper in our backpacks while maintaining a steady grip on our separate lockets. Looking each other in the eyes, we remove our wish-granters from our necks. My youth hands me hers, I hand her mine, and we both hesitate only briefly before wearing our false years' locket as our own.

The ground spins as I vault into my kindergarten self's body. I am now my small, curly-haired, bright-colored kindergarten version of myself, and she wears the disguise of my high school years. I now have her pink, butterfly backpack, and she has my navy one. Our eyes meet only for a brief moment, then without another word, I step toward the kindergarten and she steps toward the high school with this thought in mind: *"you may not forever return, or fix this trick in the slightest / until you decide that of your many years of youth, yours have been the brightest"*

6 years of youth

This is gonna be weird. *Very* weird. But more than that, it's gonna be epic! I'm a high schooler now! A big kid! An almost, kind of, sort of *grownup*! I must be ten feet tall. For however long this crazy switch lasts, I know it's going to be great.

Looking down at the pretty white shirt with flower patterns I'm now wearing, I decide the sixteen-year-old me has great fashion sense. I should for sure take her styles to use when we switch back. Or *if* we switch back. Maybe I'll never want to leave. And maybe she won't either.

I run my fingers through my long, brown hair, which is way softer than it was a minute ago. How did it turn this smooth? I've always had frizzy hair, so this is strange. Maybe the sixteen-year-old me just wears a wig. I grab a section of my hair and yank it.

"Ouch!"

I gasp at the sound of my deeper, big kid voice. Nope, no wig.

From the other side of the building, I see another big kid walking toward me. She has light red hair held in a neat bun and wears a buttoned shirt and a black skirt. The backpack she carries looks more like a suitcase. She looks at me, but doesn't smile. I know who she is within a few seconds.

It's the big kid version of Aimee! She steps toward me with a look of concern. It's the same look grownups used to give me back in daycare when I would try to eat glue.

"Jessica," she says, still not smiling.

As soon as I hear her voice, I'm even more interested in what adventures this place will bring. It's *Aimee* as a *big kid*! I wonder if she's a lot smarter now than she is in kindergarten. I wonder if she's friends with the sixteen-year-old me. And no matter how annoyingly smart she is, I can't wait to talk to her.

"You're Aimee!" I say.

"Yes," she says, nodding her head slowly. "May you inform me as to why, exactly, you were just yanking at your own hair?"

"I was just trying to see if I'm wearing a wig."

Tilting her head, she takes a step closer to me.

"But wouldn't one have previous knowledge of the fact that she is wearing a wig before yanking at her own hair?"

"Well, most of the time, yes, but— *oh, wait!*"

I remember the locket's warning and put my hand over my mouth.

"I can't tell you, can I?"

"I would ask you what it is that you are unable to tell me, but that would be illogical."

She stares at me in silence. I look at the ground, then return my eyes to her focused, somewhat scary stare.

"I, um… I have a question."

"I have thousands upon thousands of questions that, based on my infallible logic, will never have a chance of being answered in the inconceivably microscopic speck of time that is the human lifespan in combination with this society's meager quantity of attainable knowledge," she says, her voice dull.

"Um…" I say, trying to pretend I understood whatever she just said. "Alright, then. Well, my question is, where do I go for class?"

"We have trigonometry first. Today is a Day Three, don't you recall?"

"A what?"

"A Day Three."

"What's that?"

"I don't know whether you are joking or just eminently idiotic."

She stares at me as if waiting for a response, but I have no idea what she said. I also have no idea where I'm supposed to go, or how I'm supposed to get there. Or what I'm supposed to do. How I'm supposed to act…

"Okay, well, where do I find this… *tigonomy* class?"

Aimee shakes her head while looking at the ground for a second before bringing her eyes back to me.

"If you believe purposely mispronouncing the word 'trigonometry' is even remotely amusing, then you are wrong. And if your mispronunciation was indeed not purposeful, then you might want to consider undergoing a brain scan."

Panicking, I just stare at her, unable to put my thoughts into words. What if she can see through my big kid disguise? I turn around and look back at the kindergarten for just a second, then finally, she answers.

"Our trigonometry classroom is located on the third floor in room 322. The reason as to why this information appears foreign to you is prodigiously unclear to me. You act as though it's your first day here, or something of the sort."

"Ha, ha," I say, avoiding her eyes. "Okay, well… I'll see you later!"

I wave to her, but she stands still. She continues to give me a concerned look, then starts to say something. But instead, she shakes her head once again, then walks away toward the building next to the kindergarten. You know, the one where all the big kids go. The one where I don't belong.

I sit in the grass and sigh. How am I ever going to do this? I'll never be able to find anything in that big, scary building, let alone many different classes. And if I understood her right, Aimee said there are three floors? It hasn't even been five minutes, and I can already tell this is going to be more of a challenge than I thought. I still don't know what "Day Three," "Tigonomy," or most of the words Aimee said even mean. How does my sixteen-year-old self do this? Does that mean that someday, when I'm really her, I will too?

There's no way I'll be able to fit in here. I can hide in kindergarten, but not in this place. What if I have no friends as a big kid? What if I have to do this alone with only my six years? What if even Chloe doesn't like me anymore?

Feeling stressed, I look at the locket around my neck. Other than my six-year-old mind, it's the only thing that looks the same. The locket belongs to my sixteen-year-old self, but in some confusing way, she is me. So this locket is mine. My voice is now different, my hair has completely changed, I'm now tall and wear totally different clothes. But this locket is still the same.

To my surprise, my locket buzzes. When I open it, two pieces of folded paper fall out. I unfold the first one and see a schedule, but it's nothing like the ones I'm used to. It reads:

Day 3

Class 1: Trigonometry, room #322: 8:00-9:00

Class 2: English, room #209: 9:05-10:05

Class 3: History, room #204: 10:10-11:10

Class 4: Chemistry, room #111: 11:15-12:15

Lunch: 12:20-12:55

Class 5: Physical Education, Athletic Center: 1:00-2:00

This is *way* too complicated! I've never heard of most of these classes before, and I know big kids don't have teachers to tell them where to go. I'm also not sure what the numbers after the rooms are, and I don't know why class #5 has no room number, but instead says "athletic center," yet another term I don't know the meaning of. Hoping the second piece of paper will help me, I unfold it, and the same familiar voice reads:

"going to high school will be difficult at age six / to succeed, you must be aware of several tricks: / never walk in the middle of the hall / make sure to always get right back up and never cry when you fall /

you will not be able to make it through this on your own / so whenever you feel overwhelmed, just know that you will never be alone"

I put the papers in my backpack and close my locket. How are these messages appearing? It seems impossible. And who are they from? It makes no sense. None of this does. I'm watching the impossible happen before my very eyes.

"Jess!"

I hear an energetic, big kid voice call my name, then turn to see a girl running toward me. She's a little taller than my sixteen-year-old self, and has shoulder-length, wavy blonde hair. She wears a flowy purple shirt, black jeans, and way too many bracelets on both wrists. I know who she is!

"Chloe!"

"What are you doing out here? Trig starts in three minutes! Come on!"

Chloe grabs my hand and helps me up off the grass, then we run toward the front door of the big kid school. I stay behind her, and she occasionally checks back to make sure I'm still following her lead. Chloe opens the door, we both step inside, and suddenly, I'm a high schooler.

16 years of youth

This is going to be undoubtedly *amazing*!

Returning to kindergarten with the smarts of a high schooler will surely be the most fascinating experience I could ever imagine. I'll have no work actually requiring any thought, and for once, I'll be the wisest in my class. Who wouldn't want that? I sure feel bad for my six-year-old self. Being in high school with the education of a kindergartener sounds like a nightmare. Even being in high school with the education of a high schooler can be awful.

But that's her problem. She wished it upon herself.

Peering down at my neon-pink shirt and purple polka-dot pants, I cringe at how little fashion sense I had as a kindergartener. My obnoxiously yellow shoes don't pair well with the rest of my outfit, and my locket appears oversized on my small figure. I run my fingers through my frizzy, curly hair and gain a new appreciation for my high school hair routine.

Brush. Product. Straighten. Lightly curl. More product. *Lots* of product. It's a tedious practice. But I already miss my toxic fruit salad.

Once I reach the playground, I stop to sit on one of the swings. As soon as I do so, my locket buzzes. Hoping for another note bearing useful information, I open it. And sure enough, a small, folded paper falls out. It says:

should you show off as too smart, it is clear / that the benefits of this experience will begin to disappear

Well, that's no use.

Being the smartest was supposed to be the best part of this. But I suppose it would be strange if the kindergarteners were learning the alphabet and I said, "Hey guys, did you know that the Pythagorean Theorem is $a^2+b^2=c^2$?"

Perhaps I should stay at a 1st-2nd grade level to impress them. 3rd grade maximum.

I look up and see a short little girl with wavy blond hair running toward me. She waves as if we were long lost friends, and immediately, I recognize her as Chloe.

She's so cute as a kindergartener!

"Jess! What are you doing out here? Mrs. Rose is looking for you!"

I hop off the swing.

"Were you just gonna play on the playground all day? That would sure be fun. We should do that someday when we're big kids," she says with a look of timeless youth.

"Yes, we should," I say, then gasp at the sound of my higher-pitched, kindergarten voice. I have a lot to get used to. "We will never be too old for the playground."

With her leading the way, we walk toward the little building. Chloe opens a door with bright, colorful letters on it, we step inside, and suddenly, I'm a kindergartener.

3

6 years of youth

Chloe and I walk into the big kid school, and I look around in amazement. This place is huge! The halls are much longer than the ones I'm used to, and there's so many big kids talking all around us it hurts my ears. There must be a million people in this place! I recognize a few of them as the big kid versions of my classmates in kindergarten, but they're moving too fast for me to say hi. Lots of the big kids look even older than my sixteen-year-old self. I even see one with a beard!

With every second, more big kids walk inside. There are huge groups of them everywhere, so Chloe and I can't move very fast. I guess big kids don't walk in lines like we do in kindergarten. Maybe they should consider it. If this was that *other place*, anything other than neat, single-file lines would never work.

I try to move closer to Chloe so I don't lose her in the mob, but I get pushed by people trying to run. A few big kids yell to try to get past more easily, and I wonder why they don't get in trouble. Maybe it's because there are no teachers in sight. If Mrs. Rose were here, she would not be happy. No way.

After a few minutes, Chloe and I reach a set of stairs, and we walk up slowly. She's still in front of me, because she has to be the leader. Here in high school, I'm going to need her to help me keep my real years a secret. Because of my locket's message, I can't tell anyone— not even Chloe! But without a best friend, I'm sure I couldn't hide my kindergarten years for long.

"*Ugh!*" she sighs. "Could this move any slower?"

I can see how it could get annoying for the big kids, but I'm glad walking through this school takes so long. It gives me more time to look around at the place I didn't think I would find myself in for many, many years.

Once we make it to the top of the stairs, Chloe runs across the now less crowded halls. But I continue walking. If I've learned anything from kindergarten, it's that there is absolutely no running allowed in the halls. Ever. It's very dangerous. You could fall and break a few bones, you know.

"What are you *doing*, Jess?" says Chloe. "We're gonna be late!"

Trusting my best friend and all of her added years, I match her pace.

We run along the hallways until we reach a room marked #322. As soon as we walk inside, a bell rings, but I don't see one anywhere. The large group of big kids stop talking, and strangely, they stare at us as if we did something wrong.

"Don't look at us like that!" says Chloe, crossing her arms. "We're not even late, technically."

There are only two empty desks in the entire room, one in the front and one in the back. Chloe takes the one in the back, so I'm stuck sitting in front.

Looking around the room, I see many more people than there are in my kindergarten class. One teacher sits at a desk with lots of pencils and other clutter that faces the smaller desks where all the big kids sit, and he looks tired while he types something on a computer. All around the room are posters with words and symbols I don't understand, and near my desk is a window I can look through to see the much-adored playground. There's stacks of paper

EMMA MCNAMARA

everywhere, as well as a big blue bin labeled "tests." I've never taken a real test before, but I hear if you fail one, you fail school and have to live in a box.

"Please take out your homework from last night," says the teacher. Unlike Mrs. Rose, this teacher doesn't seem to smile often. He looks around the room as the big kids each get out a piece of paper, then he stares right at me.

"The homework, Jessica?"

Homework...

I've heard that word before, but Chloe tells me it's something we won't have to worry about until around second grade. I guess she didn't take into consideration I might switch my years. Everyone else has a page on their desks holding way more numbers than I have ever seen on a piece of paper before. And everyone is looking at me.

"Do you have the homework?" asks the teacher, raising his eyebrows.

"Yes?"

"Then haven't you gotten the memo you should take it out now?"

Not sure what to do, I look around at all the big kids staring at me. Many of them just look tired, but a few of them laugh and whisper to each other. Confused, I turn back to the teacher, hoping he'll explain to me what in the world is going on. Before I can panic much, a girl I don't recognize reaches into my backpack, takes out a folder, and slams a piece of paper onto my desk.

"You're welcome, idiot," she says. I wonder why the teacher doesn't yell at her. If this were kindergarten, she'd get a sticker taken away, for sure.

I look at the paper. On it are so many numbers, letters, and confusing symbols I have no idea how to even try to understand it. My sixteen-year-old self must be super smart. And I don't even know her.

36

"Now that you're all prepared, let's go over the homework questions," says the teacher. "Who would like to start with number one?"

About three people raise their hands, which I find strange. Since big kids are supposed to be smart, I thought more of them would want to answer.

"Aimee."

Of course. Aimee is the smartest in my class in kindergarten, so it's no wonder she's the smartest here in high school, too.

She waits for everyone to be completely silent, then speaks.

"The question was, 'If six squared plus ten squared equals c squared, what is the hypotenuse of the triangle?' Logically, I squared six, the outcome being 36, then I squared ten, the outcome being 100. I then added these two numbers to a result of 136. Finally, I found the square root of 136, which, rounded up to the nearest first decimal place, is 11.7."

What?!

Nobody else seems confused, but I have no idea how she did that. I tried to follow along for the first part, but as soon as the word "squared" came up, I lost it. I wonder if the sixteen-year-old me can actually understand this stuff, or if she feels just as lost as I do.

The teacher better not call on me, or I'm doomed. There's no way I'm gonna get through this whole day without the big kids finding out I'm not one of them. I'm not as cool as they are, or as special. And I'm not nearly as smart. Not even close. I feel like I'm wearing a mask that could fall off and show my kindergarten years at any second.

My locket buzzes. Confused, I open it as the teacher writes lots of numbers on a whiteboard. In it is another piece of folded paper, which I unfold to hear the familiar voice read:

"the answer is 64"

I panic and glance around the room, worried everyone just heard my locket talk. But no one even looks at me.

Not knowing what the message means, I close my locket and put the piece of paper in my backpack. The teacher continues to write on the board, then turns around to face the class.

"Who knows the answer to question six?"

Now only two people raise their hands.

"Only two of you?" He stands still with his arms crossed, looking at the class silently.

About three other people raise their hands about halfway, avoiding eye contact with him. Everyone else just looks bored.

"Jessica."

Me? I didn't sign up for this.

"Huh?"

"What is the answer to number six?"

"But I didn't raise my hand!"

"I am very much aware of that."

"B-but..." I stutter, surprised he doesn't seem to understand. "You raise your hand when you want to answer. If someone doesn't raise their hand, then they don't want to answer. You see, you're only supposed to call on someone who raises their hand."

I thought the teacher was supposed to teach me, not the other way around! I'm only in kindergarten, and even *I* know he's only supposed to call on someone if they raise their hand. He doesn't even have popsicle sticks!

A few big kids laugh, but most of them yell all at once.

"You tell him, Jess!" shouts a girl a couple of seats away from me.

"This is an injustice to all students!" says a boy on the other side of the room. "Teachers who purposely embarrass their students deserve to be fired!"

Almost all of the big kids cheer, but Aimee looks at her desk and shakes her head.

"I know what we have to do!" yells Chloe, her voice louder than any of the other big kids, even though she's all the way in the back of the room. "I declare today, February 13, National TAYFABYAPA Awareness Day! Who's with me?"

The big kids cheer again, and to try to fit in, I do the same. But I have no idea what's going on. I don't know what everyone's so excited about, and I have no idea what "TAYFABYAPA" means. I don't know anything.

The teacher looks angry, and for a second, I worry he'll take away our recess privileges. Then I remember where I am.

"Quiet down!" he yells. But nobody seems to hear him.

"When I say, 'No more,' you say 'TAYFABYAPA'!" says Chloe, standing on her desk. "No more!"

"TAYFABYAPA!"

"No more!"

"TAYFABYAPA!"

"No—"

"*Enough!*" yells the teacher. "You're disrupting our class time! But would someone please tell me what 'TAYFABYAPA' means?"

"It stands for 'Teacher Asks You For Answers Because You Aren't Paying Attention,'" says Chloe, slowly sitting back in her seat.

"I will call on whomever I want whenever I want to," says the teacher. "Now, Jessica, will you please tell us the answer to question number six?"

Oh no. There's no way I'm gonna get this right. I look at the piece of paper in front of me, but it isn't helpful. Doesn't my sixteen-year-old self know she has to put the answer in a separate box? I'm about to give up, but then I remember.

"The answer is 64."

"Very good. See, if you answer more often, you just might be right."

If only my locket could tell me everything, I'd be right all the time! But I know that's not how it works. My sixteen-year-old self is probably smart enough to know all the answers on her own.

The teacher talks on and on about things I don't understand, and we spend the rest of class solving what have to be the most complicated math problems in the history of school. There's no snack time, no change of activity, and no breaks of any kind. Just math. For an hour. As a big kid. (As a kindergartener. *Shh!*)

A loud bell rings overhead, and finally, the teacher stops talking. The big kids pack their bags and walk toward the door, so I do the same. As I follow them out of the classroom, Chloe runs toward me and gives me a high five.

"We've done well, Jess. Happy TAYFABYAPA Day!"

I smile, but I'm still confused. *TAY-FAB-YA-PA* seems strange to me, and I'm not sure what I did that Chloe gave me a high five for. Maybe it's just because of my years.

"I gotta go to my locker now," she says. "See you in English!"

As I walk through the crowded, noisy hallways, my locket buzzes again. I open it and the familiar voice reads:

"today you might have trouble finding your way around / so despite the importance of your independence, I will tell you that your next class is one floor down"

16 years of youth

I remember this place!

These halls are the same ones I walked through in neat, single-file lines ten years ago, a vision bringing back an abundance of both positive and negative memories. To my gratitude, everything is completely different to high school. Instead of a wild mass of students crowding the halls, there's a small number of parents calmly walking their children into various classrooms. Instead of being covered with pencils, crumpled paper, old food, and random school supplies, the floors are completely clean with no tripping hazards in sight. And instead of classrooms marked with numbers too small to read, there are large posters on every door with the class number, teacher's name, and words "Are you lost? No worries! Go to the Main Office near the front door for help." It all feels so calm, so friendly, so anti-stress— so not high school. Imagining the day ahead, I wish I could stay in kindergarten forever.

"Jessica, Chloe, are you lost, darlings?"

A woman with a sweet smile and soft eyes stands in front of us.

"Come with me, I'll bring you to your classroom," she says in an irritatingly high-pitched voice. "Don't you worry."

This never happens in high school.

It's only been a few minutes, and the differences between kindergarten and that *other place* are already eminently clear. When lost in the halls in high school, teachers rarely offer guidance, and I'm pretty sure they laugh at our suffering.

I already know this youth will be preferable over my own.

The woman walks with us until we reach a familiar classroom, and we stop outside the open door.

"Mrs. Rose!" she calls. "These two sweethearts got a little lost, but they're here now. They were very brave and didn't panic. I'm proud of you, girls!"

She waves to us, then walks away. Chloe and I saunter into the room, and immediately, I'm comforted by the welcoming, carefree vibe. The much-adored Mrs. Rose gives us a smile, and my false youth smiles back. Although I haven't seen her in ten years, she looks just as I remember. Her pigmented, rose-gold hair, her bright pink cheeks, her amiable smile; everything about her is exactly as I remember from when I was truly six years old. She motions for me and Chloe to join the rest of the kindergarteners, who sit cross-legged in a circle on the floor.

"I am so proud of you two for not panicking when you got lost," she says, standing up from her chair and walking toward a file cabinet. "You both get a sticker!"

I get a sticker for getting lost? In high school that earns you a tardy slip. If I forget my homework, will I also get a sticker for not crying about it? Oh wait— I'm in kindergarten. There *is* no homework to forget about! I could get used to this. There's no cruel teachers, no tests, no stress of any kind. Just fun. For the whole day. As a kindergartener. (As a high schooler. *Shh!*)

Mrs. Rose hands me a purple star sticker, and for Chloe, a pink smiley face. Chloe puts hers on her nose, so I do the same. I look around to see the kindergarteners staring at us with narrowed eyes and crossed arms.

"Today, we're going to learn more math!" says Mrs. Rose, pausing as if anticipating some sort of reaction. A few kindergarteners appear at least mildly interested. "We will review the numbers up to twenty, the concept of 'more or less' and later today, we will learn addition!"

She sets out a box of colorful, connectable cubes, and my brain is bombarded with an abundance of bright memories.

"This is one cube," she says unnecessarily slowly, holding up a bright blue cube. "And this is two, then three. Most of you already know that. But would someone like to tell me how many this is?"

She adds one more to a paper plate, and I raise my hand promptly.

"Four."

But of course, I can't stop there. This is kindergarten, after all. And I'm sixteen.

"Then if you add another, it's five, then six, then if you add ten more it's sixteen, then if you triple it—"

"*Woah*, Jessica!" says Mrs. Rose, mouth agape. The kindergarteners look at me with wide eyes. "I'm impressed you know all that, but you need to give somebody else a turn."

Somebody else? Oh, right. Somebody who's actually a kindergartener. Somebody who's not sixteen. Mrs. Rose puts four more cubes on the plate, then looks at the class.

"Who would like to tell me how many I have now?"

A few kids count the cubes on their fingers, but the rest of the class doesn't even try. After a few moments, a girl I recognize as Mindi, one of the popular students in high school, raises her hand.

"There are eight cubes."

"Very good, Mindi!" says Mrs Rose. She adds two more. "How many do I have now?"

The girl next to Mindi, who I recognize as Laura, raises her hand. For as long as I've known them, Laura plays the role of a ruthless villain, and Mindi is the timid sidekick who would rather not participate in any trouble. But when Mindi tries to get away, Laura always manages to draw her back in.

"You have nine," says Laura with an arrogant little grin.

"Almost, sweetie, just one more."

Some kids laugh, and Laura's face turns a deep red. If I was actually in kindergarten, in my true years, I think I would laugh at her too. But I'd like to think I'm more mature as a high schooler.

"Oh, yeah, I meant ten. I was just joking," she says, and most of the kindergarteners seem to believe her. "Can I have a sticker?"

"I'm sorry, sweetie, but you don't get a sticker if you ask for one. Asking for a prize is rude, but you did a great job answering!"

Laura's mouth falls wide open. She clenches her fists, lips trembling.

43

"WAHHH!"

It sounds like she's crying, but no tears are visible. Mindi avoids eye contact.

"I'm sorry, Laura," says Mrs. Rose, getting up from her chair to give Laura a hug. "You're right; you do deserve a sticker."

Mrs. Rose reaches into the file cabinet, and while her back is turned, Laura looks over at Mindi with a grin of pure evil. That little liar! I sure feel bad for my six-year-old self. Being in kindergarten with Laura and Mindi must be a nightmare. Unless you have the mind of a high schooler, that is.

Mrs. Rose returns with a green and pink sticker in the shape of a flower, which is way cooler than my purple star sticker. Laura takes a piece of paper out of her pocket and places the sticker on it, along with the dozens of others she seems to have collected.

"Now we are going to quickly review 'more or less,' but I think most of you already know what those mean. Who would like to explain?"

I raise my hand along with three other people: Chloe, Aimee, and a boy sitting across from me. The boy has dark brown hair, bronze skin, and wears a colorful cartoon t-shirt with blue jeans. I recognize him immediately, and I can't help but smile as Mrs. Rose calls—

"Rye."

Rye answers in the adorable kindergarten voice of his I haven't heard in ten years.

"More is when you have a lot of something, and less is when you have a little of something."

"Very good! So, Rye, if I have three apples, and, let's say, Jessica has five, who has more?"

He looks across the circle at me and smiles.

"Jess has more."

"Good job! If I have five apples and Rye has three, who has *less*?"

44

I raise my hand hastily.

"Rye has less."

"Very good! We have five minutes until recess, so let's see what you've learned. I know you all know your numbers, so we'll review 'more or less,' which should be easy!" says Mrs. Rose as if it were the most exciting concept in the world. But who am I to judge? I'm the new one here.

Mrs. Rose takes out a cup filled with popsicle sticks, and more memories from my real days of kindergarten return to me. She takes out a name.

"Chloe. If I have two apples and you have four, who has more?"

"I have more!"

One by one, Mrs. Rose goes through the cup of popsicle sticks until only the high schooler is left. Everyone has answered correctly, and I'm confident I can do the same. I did pass kindergarten, after all.

"Well, Jessica, it looks like you're last today," says Mrs. Rose. "Everyone, make sure to be nice if she gets it wrong. There's a lot of pressure answering last."

Pressure in kindergarten? I don't think so. At least not for a sixteen-year-old.

"If you have six apples and I have two, who has less?"

And I was wrong. The whole class is staring at me, and even though I have a mind ten years older than them, I still feel pressure. Maybe there are parts of me that just won't change with altered years.

"You have less."

"Excellent, Jessica! You kids get a well-deserved extra five minutes of playtime."

The kindergarteners cheer as Mrs. Rose lines us up by the door to go outside for recess. Rye approaches me, and however childish it may sound, I get butterflies.

"Nice job, Jess!" he says with a shy smile.

He gives me a high five, and I think I'm ten years past in love.

4

6 years of youth

When I make it to the second floor, I look for a sign to tell me where to find room 209. That's where my class called "English" is supposed to be, but I'm not sure why the big kid me has to learn that. Chloe tells me big kids get to learn new languages, but learning the same one I already know doesn't seem to have a point. Maybe she just reads books in that class, kind of like when Mrs. Rose reads to us in kindergarten. Or maybe in this strange place, nothing is the same.

This is going to be harder than I thought.

The numbers on the classroom doors are so small I can barely see them, so I try to get closer, which is nearly impossible with all the people. This place seems to be designed to make everyone confused! Trying to read the numbers, I crash into one big kid, then nearly trip over another while I'm apologizing to the first. It takes forever to find 209, and when I walk into the classroom, I see a woman with a stern face and a pair of glasses that look too big for her eyes. She's reading something silently at the front of the room, and groups of big kids sit at desks and talk about whatever it is big kids talk about. Most of them sit toward the back, so I think I'll do the same. If I act like a big kid, I don't think anyone will notice there's something different about me. I'm still Jessica Jule Locke. Only my years have changed.

In the back row of desks, I sit next to a girl I don't recognize. I don't think she's the big kid version of anyone I know from kindergarten, but she seems nice enough. Maybe I could talk to her, and maybe this won't be so different after all, and maybe—

"No."

I turn toward the girl, and when I do, her eyes are already on me.

"No what?"

"You can't sit there!"

"Why not?"

What if she knows about my years? What if she says no kindergarteners are allowed here? Worst of all, what if she says I'm just too stupid to be in this school?

"That's Chelsea's seat," she says, rolling her eyes. "What, do you think you're the queen of this class?"

"I don't think I'm the queen of anything."

"Then why would you sit in Chelsea's seat?"

"I don't know!" I say. But I'm sure the big kid me would have. "So we have assigned seats?"

Mrs. Rose only gives us assigned seats when we don't behave. Other than the time-out chair, it's for sure the worst punishment.

"Only wannabe class queens who think it's cool to never shut up have assigned seats, like that blond best friend of yours."

I think she's talking about Chloe, but like with almost everything so far today, I'm not sure. Maybe the high school me has more than one best friend. But if she's anything like me, that's not likely.

"Okay, well… where am I supposed to sit?"

The rude girl points to a seat in the middle of the second row of desks, and even though I'm still confused, I pick up my backpack and move. As more big kids enter the classroom, they sit and talk loudly with each other. I recognize a few as the older versions of kids I know from kindergarten. There's Laura and Mindi behind me near the rude girl who wouldn't let me sit next to her. I see Aimee at the other side of the room, and Chloe seems to have an assigned seat next to her. But other than that, I'm clueless.

After another minute, the teacher stands up and talks to the class, and right away, I know she is not like Mrs. Rose. She doesn't seem as friendly or as energetic, and just like my last teacher, I don't think she would be happy to know a six-year-old is in her class. But if I can be at least a little smart, I don't think she'll find out.

"Today we'll continue reading Shakespeare's masterpiece, *Romeo and Juliet*. Please take out your copies now."

I open my big kid backpack and search for a book, which is easy to find thanks to my well-organized sixteen-year-old self. I put it on my desk and wait as several other people in the class struggle to find theirs.

Moving her eyes around the room and giving stern looks to the few people who seem to not be able to find their books, the teacher tells us to turn to page 46. And I try to relax. Unlike my first class in my false years, I'm not the one in trouble with the teacher. Maybe that only happens once a day in high school. Or maybe I'm just hopelessly hopeful.

"Before we begin, please take out the reading comprehension questions you were assigned to complete on our previous section for homework."

Oh, no. Not that word again.

This is only my second class as a big kid, and already there's homework in both? This would never happen in kindergarten. But I'm not yet ready to regret my wish. This time, there's no need to panic. I know where to find this *homework*. I open my backpack and take out the folder that had my sixteen-year-old self's homework in my last class, and look around to see everyone else doing the same.

Inside is the homework with all the numbers, and a piece of paper with a combination of letters, numbers, and different symbols. Since it's my only option, I take out the worksheet with "2na(s) + cl2(g) → 2nacl(s)" written in neat handwriting. Something about it doesn't seem right, but then again, something about my years feel the same way. So this should be fine. Maybe the teacher won't even notice.

Just as I worried, there's a piece of paper on everyone's desk that looks completely different than mine. Hoping to blend in with the big kids, I pretend nothing is wrong. Then I look up to see the teacher staring at me.

"What is this, Jessica?"

"My homework?"

"This isn't chemistry class."

"Isn't what?"

The class goes silent. The big kids look at me, and the teacher seems annoyed and angry at the same time. I fill with the familiar feeling of panic, a feeling that seems a regular part of high school.

"Did you do the homework, Jessica?" she asks, crossing her arms.

Just to make sure, I ask a question I already know the sad answer to.

"This isn't the homework?"

I hear laughter all around me.

"There is no chemistry in *Romeo and Juliet*," says the teacher. Then she pauses. "Correction: there is chemistry in *Romeo and Juliet*. But most certainly not this kind."

She points at the piece of paper I have out on my desk, which I quickly put back into my folder. As I put my folder into my backpack, I feel anger toward the sixteen-year-old me. How could she be so stupid? Maybe we aren't as different as I thought.

"So I take it you don't have the homework?"

"No," I say softly, looking at the ground.

She shakes her head and writes something on a clipboard.

"That is very disappointing, Jessica. As a sophomore student in an honors level English class, the expectation is—"

"Please don't put me in the time-out chair!"

The silence in the room somehow gets softer, and the screaming in my head gets louder with every second. The big kids stare at me with wide eyes, and a few seconds later, I realize my mistake.

"I, um... nevermind."

Instead of responding, the teacher joins the awkward silence, a quiet I now realize will be a regular part of being six in high school. She then walks away from my desk and speaks to all of the big kids. And the little one, of course.

"Please follow along as I read the opening monologue."

Other than only being able to understand a few words of whatever strange language the book is in, this isn't too different from reading time in kindergarten. There's no pictures in the book, and we're at desks instead of in a circle on the floor, but I barely notice. Just like reading time in kindergarten, I can easily daydream without being caught not paying attention, and I don't have to do any work. So I give up on trying to follow along, and I think about rainbows and recess while still holding my book open. After a few minutes of reading, the teacher closes her book.

"Before we continue, I want you all to turn to someone next to you and discuss what we just read."

This is weird. Mrs. Rose only asks us to talk about what we read as a class, not partners. But Mrs. Rose isn't here. And neither are the picture books.

Most of the big kids turn to someone next to them and start talking right away, and I soon realize we won't be assigned partners. I try to get the attention of a few people around me, but they're all talking with someone else. Someone who's not six. Chloe looks at me from the other side of the room, and I give her a smile like everything is normal. Just as I'm about to give up, a girl in front of me turns around.

"You can join us, Jess," she says with a smile.

Within a few moments of looking at her, I realize I know her from kindergarten. It's Kayla, the nice one, sitting next to Kora, the other nice one! They look so similar that when I first met them in Mrs. Rose's class, I thought they were sisters, and they're so kind to everyone they make Laura and Mindi look like total monsters. As big kids, they both have long brown hair held in ponytails, and their outfits match perfectly. They look similar now to how they do in kindergarten, unlike my true years and my big kid self. Maybe years don't change a person as much as I thought. Or maybe I just don't follow the rules of age.

"We're not actually gonna talk about *Romeo and Juliet*," says Kayla quietly. They both laugh. "It's so stupid. I don't even understand what any of the characters are saying."

They don't understand it? But they're big kids! *Real* big kids!

"How's your day going, Jess?" asks Kora. "I'm sure it's more interesting than this class."

"Um... it's been interesting, for sure."

"*Oooh*, how are things going with Rye?"

Rye. Rye Arthur. Of course, I know who she's talking about, but I'm not sure why she would ask me that. Rye and I don't talk much in kindergarten, but maybe it's different in high school. It seems like there's a lot about the big kid me I don't know. Maybe everything's different.

"With Rye? What do you—"

"Now we'll continue reading," says the teacher, interrupting our conversation about definitely not the book. I wonder if all big kids break the rules. "Who would like to participate in reading this scene?"

Only two people volunteer.

"Kayla," says the teacher, even though she didn't raise her hand. "You will be reading for Juliet."

Before she has time to respond, Chloe stands from the other side of the room. She doesn't look happy, and in kindergarten, when Chloe isn't happy, she makes sure everyone knows it.

"We will not accept this! Today, Tuesday, February 13, is TAYFABYAPA Awareness Day. No more TAYFABYAPA!"

Almost all of the big kids cheer, and many chant, "No more TAYFABYAPA!" with even more energy than when this happened last class. Trying to fit in, I chant along with them, because I think that's what the older me would do. I have no idea why this is such a big deal. Nothing this crazy ever happens in kindergarten.

"Quiet down!" yells the teacher. Unlike last class, everyone goes silent right away. "Now, what in the world does *TAY-FAB-YA-PA* mean?"

"It stands for 'Teacher Asks You For Answers Because You Aren't Paying Attention," says Chloe, a proud look on her face. Then she looks at me and smiles. "Jess and I came up with it earlier this semester."

Jess and I? Oh, right. The *other* Jess. The cool one. The smart one. The old one.

"First of all, I asked you to read, not to supply answers, rendering your pitiful acronym useless in this situation. Secondly, I am absolutely *flabbergasted* you believe this is acceptable behavior. And thirdly, be quiet! I don't want to give anyone a detention."

All of those big words make me feel even smaller, but all of the big kids seem to understand. I'm not sure what "detention" means, but it must be pretty scary. Maybe what I've heard about all high school teachers being mean is true.

"Now that we're done with these shenanigans, who else would care to read?"

This time, a few more people volunteer, and the teacher tells each of them a name. Even though I don't raise my hand, she gives me the name "Nurse." After what just happened, there's no way I'll argue with her. Besides, I bet I'll only need to read when one of the characters gets sick. So until then, I can just relax and listen to everyone else.

After about five minutes of reading, the classroom fills with silence. A bad sign. I look up from the book I was definitely not following along with, and once again, the teacher is staring at me.

"Jessica."

"Huh?"

"Please don't respond with 'huh,' it makes you sound idiotic. Now, Jessica?"

"W-what?"

"It's your turn to read!"

Oh, no. I should have known this would happen. I have no idea what page we're on, I already forgot the name of the book, and based off what I've heard so far, there's no way I'll be able to pronounce any of the words correctly. Lucky locket, please don't fail me now! But my locket doesn't buzz, and my heart beats faster with every second.

"We're waiting, Jessica."

Kayla turns around and picks up my book, then flips to a page and points to a section. She hands it back to me, and in my state of panic, I just stare at it. It doesn't take long before I reach a decision: nope. There is no way I'm going to be able to do this. I don't want to. I can't. I won't. And I know how to get out of this. It's quite simple, actually. It works every time.

"WAHHH!"

Although my cry starts as fake, as soon as I think about being stuck here, my tears become real. At least I made it through my first class and part of this one without crying. For me with my six years, that's impressive.

All of the big kids look at me with wide eyes, and again, a few laugh. But to my surprise, the teacher doesn't come over to give me a hug. She offers no stickers, no comfort, and no smiles. All she gives me is a look of confusion. I wonder why— *oh, yeah*. I forgot. Big kids don't cry. Ever. No matter how upset they are, no big kid is allowed to cry. Well, this is awkward.

"Um..." I say, looking around at all the faces judging me and my false years. "I... um... I bit my tongue. Yes, that's it! Sorry."

Even though I think my explanation was pretty convincing, nobody takes their eyes away from me, and the teacher shakes her head and crosses her arms once again. The silence hurts my ears until finally, to my relief, a bell rings overhead, and I run out of class.

I don't know why I ever made this wish. I was so stupid.

16 years of youth

I don't know why I didn't wish for this years ago!

Going back to kindergarten has been one of the best decisions I have ever made. It's like a vacation, but *so* much better. This false youth surpasses any of my days of high school in my true years, and I've only been six for a little over sixty minutes. For the first time ever, I'm the smartest in my class. Next active learning time, I'll try to show off as even smarter. I'll show Aimee what it's like not to be number one for a change.

My wish was made by sixteen years of stupid, but my sharp-witted decision has transformed me into a six-year-old genius.

We walk in a neat, single-file line out of the classroom, through the hallways, and outside for recess. The air is only a tad chilly, because even in February, it never gets too cold here in California.

And in the summer, it's never too warm. The weather is perfect, just like my years.

Once we're a couple yards away from the playground, Mrs. Rose blows a whistle and everyone bolts forward.

There are a few other classes here as well. It looks like there's about fifty kindergarteners. I recognize several of them as the younger versions of people I know from high school, but so far, I don't see any of my friends. Chloe won't be at recess since, instead, most days her parents made her take an extra class with a different teacher. Back then, I didn't think much of this, but now that I have ten more years of wisdom, I wonder why her parents couldn't have just let their kid be a kid.

And I wonder why my six years of youth wouldn't let herself be a kid.

I make my way toward the swings, but quickly turn around at the mob of crazy kindergarteners fighting over them. I then walk toward the slides and monkey bars, but seeing those crowded and chaotic as well, I back away. The seesaw seems fun, but wouldn't be functional with just one person. And from what I remember from actual kindergarten, the tire swing is a spinning wheel of danger. There's a group of boys playing frisbee in the grass, which, out of all my options, sounds the most appealing right now. But I know if I try to join them, they'll tell me "no girls allowed." And despite the anti-stress of kindergarten, I'm far too tired to try and convince them otherwise. I see a group of girls playing jump rope, and I start toward them, but turn around upon remembering the sad truth. I haven't jumped rope in many years. I'll end up falling and getting laughed at by a bunch of five and six-year-olds.

I decide to just sit on the playground bench. I'm far too old for this, anyways.

Looking at the sky, I see the faint glow of a rainbow, but when I blink, it vanishes.

I hesitantly glance at the high school next door, and I don't miss a thing. My six-year-old self is probably in the middle of class right now, while I sit here relaxing. She's probably going to ask, "When's recess?" and cry upon remembering she's a "big kid" now. She'll probably ponder why she didn't get a sticker for answering a question right, if she's ever brave enough to raise her hand. Then again, I doubt my six-year-old self would be able to answer a high school question correctly. Today will be her first experience with real work, stress, and actual school. By the end, she'll know actual school doesn't include recess or playtime. She'll probably regret ever wanting to switch, and dread the future.

Two girls walk toward me. Within a few moments, I recognize them as Kayla and Kora. They're the type of people who couldn't be mean to anyone if they tried, and it seems like they're friends with almost everyone they come across. Even in high school, they're always nice to me. From what I've seen, Kayla and Kora are almost exactly the same. In high school, they both have long, straight brown hair they wear up in a hair tie every single day. They both refuse to wear green, and they spread smiles everywhere they go. They never appear lost in life, even though they're only sixteen. The pair is always in perfect sync. As individuals, and especially as best friends, they're simply perfect. Their lives are more put together than mine will ever be. Here in kindergarten, these qualities appear unchanged. I could learn a thing or two from them.

"Hey, Jess!" says Kayla, waving at me. "Wanna play on the monkey bars with us?"

I smile and agree, but before we get to them, Rye calls out to me.

"Hey, Jess!" he says. "Wanna go on the seesaw with me?"

"Sure," I say without a hint of hesitancy.

Kayla and Kora stare at me with wide eyes.

"You're gonna leave us for a *boy*?"

"That is correct," I say, even though my six-year-old self would never. Kayla and Kora turn toward the monkey bars without me, and I sit on the seesaw with Rye and immediately engage in conversation.

"You were smart in class today," he says.

"Thanks."

"How many numbers can you count up to?"

"I don't know. If I had a lot of time, I could count up to the thousands. And I can also count in Spanish. *Uno, dos, tres*, and so on."

"Wow," he says. "What's your favorite word?"

"Flabbergasted."

"What does that mean?"

"Surprised."

"Then why don't you just say 'surprised?'"

"Because saying 'flabbergasted' is more fun."

"You have really pretty hair."

"Thanks!"

"What's your favorite number?"

"38."

"That makes sense. Because from the moment I saw you, I knew you were *surely great*."

"Aw, thanks!"

"Get it? Because *38* rhymes with *surely great*?"

"I got it," I say, unable to help but laugh.

"What's so funny?"

"You're very cute. And funny."

"Thanks! Do you wanna play together at recess more often?"

"Did you just ask me out on a date?" I ask, curious to see his reaction.

He looks confused, yet intrigued.

"Yes. Yes, I would," I say.

"Cool! So… do you like cheese?"

"Very much so."

"What's your favorite kind?"

"There's nothing better than cheddar."

"I like blue cheese. You see, most cheese is just yellow, but blue cheese is both yellow and blue."

"That's exactly what I like about you. You see, most boys here think it's not cool to talk to girls, but here you are talking with me."

"Woah!" says Rye, blushing. "You *like* something about me?"

"You bet your blue cheese."

"That's awesome! I like you too. Someday, when we're big kids, you could be my *girlfriend*."

"Did you just ask me out on a date?"

Once again, he's at a loss for words.

"Yes. Yes, I could. Our couple name would be 'Ryjess,' because thinking about you makes me out*Ryjess*ly happy."

Chloe came up with that about a year ago, and we've used it ever since.

"Our what?"

I try to think of a response, but before I can speak, one of the teachers around the playground blows a whistle, and the kindergarteners run toward a cluster of teachers.

"I'll tell you later," I say, and together we run toward the group.

After everyone is off the playground, we form a neat, single-file line and walk back inside the building. Once we're in the classroom, we sit in a circle on the carpeted floor again. I sit next to Chloe, and Rye sits directly across from me. Mrs. Rose looks around at the kindergartens, and her sole high school student, of course.

"Time for social skills!"

5

<u>6 years of youth</u>

I think I have some serious skills.

So far, I've been a high schooler for a couple of hours, and I'm still alive and well. Kind of. Crying like the little kid I am in the middle of class wasn't smart, but so far, that's been the worst of it.

My next class is supposed to be in room 204, but when I get there, the classroom is empty.

"Jess!" yells Chloe. "What are you *doing*? History starts in two minutes!"

I follow her as she runs past groups of big kids. We walk down the crowded stairway, then across a hall until, strangely, we walk into room 104 just before the bell rings. The big kids talk to one another while a teacher with a long blond ponytail and blue overalls sits reading something at a desk in the front of the room. She looks too young to be a teacher, but then again, I'm too young to be a high schooler. I sit next to Chloe in the middle of the room.

"How come the schedule says room 204, but class is actually in room 104?"

"It's just a typo. She told us that at the beginning of the year," she says, raising an eyebrow. "Are you okay, Jess? You've been acting weird today."

"Yeah," I say, trying to keep my voice from shaking. "I'm fine."

Fine. Fine, except I have to be in high school with the mind of a six-year-old. Fine, except there's nothing I want more than recess and stickers right now, but big kids don't get either. Fine, except I'm already regretting my wish to change, even if that change was just from my six-year-old self to sixteen. Young to old.

So sure, I'm fine. Except, my years are lost.

The teacher stands in front of the class, and everyone stops talking right away.

"I have to run off to a meeting, so you will have a substitute today. Please be kind."

There have been substitute teachers in kindergarten a couple of times before, and when there is, everyone gets even crazier than usual. And these are big kids. Everyone knows big kids are crazy. I wonder if my sixteen-year-old self fits that rule.

As the teacher walks toward the door, an old man with a shirt that says, "History is Fun!" walks in with more energy than I'd ever expect from someone so old.

"Don't worry, I'll make sure they behave," he says.

After the teacher leaves, most of the big kids start talking loudly.

"Quiet down!" says the substitute.

Nobody responds.

"Quiet!"

Nothing.

He takes a whistle out of his pocket and blows, silencing the class right away.

"I know your teacher has a packet of work for you all to do, but that's no fun, now is it? So how about I play an animated movie on the Revolutionary War instead?"

The big kids cheer, so I do the same. They all seem surprised, which is exactly how I feel.

"What do you kids look so surprised for? Just because I'm old, you think I'll be cranky and sour?" he asks, setting up the projector. "I'm young for my age."

16 years of youth

I'm very old for my age.

Us five and six-year-olds saunter inside and sit in a circle for social skills. If I was my high school self right now, I'm pretty sure I would be in history class with two hours of work and one hour to do it. I would be one of the dumbest in my class, and every minute would feel like forever. I would be trapped.

Instead, I'm sitting amongst a circle of kindergarteners, complimentary juice box in hand. I'm easily the smartest one here, and so far, today has felt like one giant break. Remembering the message from my locket, I smile. *"You may not forever return, or fix this trick in the slightest / until you decide that of your many years of youth, yours have been the brightest."* Mine. My sixteen years of youth as my sixteen-year-old self. The real me. There is no way I will want to go back anytime soon.

I yearn to stay here in kindergarten, even though I am starting to miss Chloe as her energetic, sixteen-year-old self. I miss our inside jokes, our deep conversations in between classes. I'm sure if I too had the mind of a six-year-old right now, we would have plenty to talk about. But I guess she's just not interested in the same things as high school Chloe.

Sitting in the circle of kindergarteners, I do feel less stressed, but out of place. I soon find myself staring at Rye, and I immediately miss him. I miss the high school version of him, the one who actually knows "Ryjess" is a thing. The one who brings me coffee right before our first class starts just because, the one who always has a pile of lame jokes to make me laugh. Sitting here in kindergarten, life is easy, but easy can turn boring quickly. There in high school, I usually feel stressed and over my head with work.

Part of me wants to stay young forever, yet my years have an aversion to restriction. My youth is uneasy about losing its title.

"Listen up, everyone!" says Mrs. Rose. "To start off social skills, we are all going to go around the circle and ask two questions to your classmates. I'll start. Laura, what did you do during recess?"

"Mindi and I got swings today," she says, looking extensively proud. "We ran so fast we beat everyone to them!"

"That sounds fun!" says Mrs. Rose, but I can't tell if her smile is as true as it appears. I have no idea what's true anymore. "After each response, you will say, 'Thanks for sharing.' On the count of three: one, two, three..."

"Thanks for sharing!" say the kids. I'm far too old to participate.

"I'll ask my second question to someone different," says Mrs. Rose. "Who did you play with during recess, Jessica?"

"Rye," I say without thinking.

The kindergarteners perk up, whispers filling the air. Rye blushes, but then smiles.

"Just because I'm a boy and she's a girl, doesn't mean we can't be friends," he says. "Jess is great, and nice, and smart, and she likes cheese, so she's awesome!"

The other boys in the class stare at him fixedly, and a few of the girls look at me with what appears to be envy. The kindergarteners half-heartedly thank us for sharing, and Mrs. Rose claps her hands.

"Great job, Rye! I totally agree with you. Who would like to ask the next two questions?"

Almost everyone's hand goes up, and Mrs. Rose calls on Chloe.

"Jess, who in this class do you think would be most likely to rule the world?"

"Rye."

"Why?"

"Because he's awesome," I say, sounding as illogical as a kindergartener in love.

Most of the kids laugh, but Rye smiles.

"I have a question for Jess," he says. "Do you want to be my friend? Even though you're a girl?"

Oh, the questions that come with youth, both false and true. Do I want to be his friend? Here in kindergarten, my years say yes. There in high school, they know ten years more.

"I would be delighted to be your friend."

I'm sure my younger years would feel the same.

"You guys are adorable!" says Mrs. Rose. "What is your second question, Rye?"

He peers across the circle at me.

"Do you want my gingerbread cookie at lunch? My mom made it."

I smile, and can only think of one logical response to such a kind offer.

"You bet your blue cheese."

6 Years of Youth

I bet the big kid me is bored in kindergarten.

Nothing interesting ever happens in Mrs. Rose's class, and other than Chloe, almost no one talks to me. I bet, with so many years, the big kid me will never learn anything in the class where I should be.

A rainbow has many more colors than the ones we can see, just like her added age is invisible with her little kid disguise. But unlike the layers of a rainbow, her years will never be as neat and pretty as art. I see her sixteen years as a blob of beautiful colors that mix and make an ugly shade, a shade no one could ever see in a rainbow.

According to my schedule, I have Chemistry class in Room 111. There are strange-looking tables at the back of the room, and a sink near the front unlike any I've seen.

As I watch more and more people walk into the room, I see a strangely familiar big kid with brown hair and a blue, buttoned shirt. He looks confident and happy, as if nothing could ever make him frown.

He's the big kid version of Rye! I was hoping to see him today. He walks toward me with a smile, and I smile back.

"Hey, Jess!" he says, sitting at the desk next to me.

He looks a lot different as a big kid. His perfect hair, his bright smile, his hazel eyes; he's like homemade cookies in human form. Perfect. I'm not sure why he would want to sit next to me, but I'm happy he does.

"Hi," I say, playing with my long, smooth hair I'm still not used to. He stares at me with a look I can't describe, and unlike me, he doesn't seem nervous or confused.

"How's your day going? Any improvement from this morning?"

He's talking to me! Me and all my six years! He says hi to me sometimes in kindergarten, but now he's a big kid. So it's different.

"Um... I'm doing pretty swell," I say, and remembering what I've learned from social skills in kindergarten, I continue the conversation. "How are you?"

"Right now, I'm grand. I'm glad to see you're feeling better, my *Valentine*."

Valentine? Why would he call me that? Why— *wait...*

Tomorrow's Valentine's Day. So could Rye Arthur be *my* Valentine? Does my sixteen-year-old self have a *boyfriend*? Yes! It makes perfect sense! He smiled at me the other day in kindergarten, he sat next to me during learning time; yes, of course he's the sixteen-year-old me's boyfriend!

"*Woah!*" I say. "I have a *boyfriend*!"

"Yes," he says, laughing a little. "I'm very much aware of that. And I'm lucky enough to have a beautiful girlfriend."

"That's me!" I say, pointing to my big kid self.

He continues to laugh, then a teacher with a white beard reminding me of Santa Claus walks into the room.

"Today we will be starting our chemical reaction lab," he says. "I'll allow you to pick your own partner for this one, so please do so now."

The big kids pair up, and Rye looks at me.

"Will you, Jessica Jule Locke, do me the great honor of being my lab partner?"

I see Chloe on the other side of the room, but she seems to be working with someone else. She's always told me I have to wait until I'm a big kid to talk to boys, so I guess now is my chance.

"Um... okey-dokey, artichokey," I say, because it's the only reply I can think of. I feel my face turn red, and Rye laughs a little, once again. I must be pretty funny.

We move from the desks to the bigger, strange-looking tables on the other side of the room. There's a bunch of weirdly-shaped objects I don't recognize, and on the wall is a red button with a sign that says, "DO NOT TOUCH THE RED BUTTON."

The teacher walks around handing out packets of paper.

"These are your lab packets. Remember to correctly follow procedures and adhere to safety precautions. I will get you your lab trays momentarily. Please get your lab coats and safety goggles now."

"I'll get it," says Rye. He walks to a cabinet in the corner of the room and comes back with two white jackets and funny-looking goggles, which he puts on. I put on the white coat just like a regular jacket, and place the goggles around my head and over my eyes, which is a lot more uncomfortable than it might seem. I stare at Rye and smile at how funny he looks.

"You have a nice face, even with weird goggles on."

Rye laughs, but I don't know why. Maybe it's because little kids are funnier than big kids. Big kids get to be smarter, cooler, more independent; six-year-olds should at least get to win at being funny.

"Same to you," he says.

The teacher puts a tray of unfamiliar objects and bright fluids on our table. Neon-yellow stickers with the word "CAUTION" are on many of the materials, along with a sign reading "WARNING" and a bunch of other words I can't be bothered to pay attention to.

"This looks dangerous," I say. Nothing this crazy would ever be allowed in kindergarten.

"We got this," says Rye. He opens his packet of papers. "Step one: apply safety goggles and lab coat. Check. Step two: fill a 150 milliliter beaker halfway with water. Be right back."

He goes to one of the many normal-looking sinks at the back of the room and fills the container halfway with water. When he returns to the table, for a second, I almost forget my years are fake.

"Step three: use tweezers to pick up one small piece of sodium. That's this," he says, pointing to small pieces of silver solid on the tray. "Carefully place the small piece of sodium in the water, then immediately back away. Would you like to do the honors?" he asks, handing me the tweezers. To be honest, I'd way rather just watch him do the lab. If I do anything, I'll probably do it wrong. But I've seen my mom use tweezers on her eyebrows before, so I know what to do.

"Sure," I say. "Let's hope I don't mess this up."

"I believe in you," he says. But I'm not sure if I do.

Looking at the big kids all around me, my heart beats faster. But out of all the challenges I've faced today, and all of those to come, this shouldn't be too bad. Using the tweezers, I pick up a small piece of the silver-colored solid, place it in the water, then back away. The water makes a sizzling noise, and what looks like steam shoots up. I don't know how, but the water turns pink, and the piece of sodium moves around the container.

"That's such a pretty color," I say, bothered by an itch near my eye, but too interested in the amazing experiment to scratch it.

Curious about all the different colorful liquids and solids on the table, I run my fingers through a yellow, powdery substance in a small bowl on the tray.

"You might not want to touch that, Jess," says Rye.

"Why?" I ask, jumping back from the table and quickly wiping my hand on my lab coat.

"Well, humans consume sulfur every day in the form of protein and such— you know, like we learned last unit. But it's better to avoid contact with the skin because some people have allergic reactions, and—"

"So that's bad?"

"You're fine," he says, smiling. "Just don't mix any of the other elements; we don't want anything to explode."

Relieved, I take off my goggles to scratch the itch near my eye. As soon as I do so, my eye feels like it's on fire.

"Jess, don't—"

"*AHHH!* It burns!"

I hear footsteps running from the front of the room, then a hand guides me forward as all the big kids become completely silent. Through my burning eyes, I see the yellow bowl in the corner of the classroom that kind of looks like a sink. The teacher rinses my eyes with water from the sink, which, for a second, makes the pain worse. I close my eyes.

"Open your eyes, Jessica!"

I do so, and then finally, the pain cools down. After what feels like forever, the water is turned off, and I lift my head. None of the big kids are working on their labs anymore. They're all staring at me. My face and hair are soaking wet, and I feel like crying, but I know I can't. I'm a high schooler now, a high schooler with a mind six years old. Right now, I feel as stupid as a toddler.

"And that, everyone, is what we have an eyewash for," says the teacher. "Now, someone please tell me, what in the world just happened?"

"She somehow managed to get sulfur in her eyes," says Aimee. She was sitting at a table next to me, and is now slowly shaking her head.

"Oh, the idiocy of teenagers these days," says the teacher quietly. Then he faces me. "Don't take that personally."

As a little girl who's not even close to actually being sixteen, I don't mind. But I'm sure my sixteen-year-old self would. Rye starts to walk toward me, but Chloe steps in front of him.

"I got this, Rye!" she says. "Come on, Jess, let's get you cleaned up."

Chloe leads me out of the classroom to a bathroom way bigger than the ones in kindergarten. I look into the mirror and gasp. My hair is now soaking wet and starting to poof up, looking more like the hair belonging to my real years. The powder has left a bright yellow stain on my white shirt, my eyes are puffy and red, and what looks like black paint is running down my cheeks.

And my birthmark. I can see it now. I can barely see it.

I scratch my left cheek and look down at my hand to see a weird cream the color of my skin under my nails.

My birthmark. I can see it now. It looks even worse on my big kid face.

"What happened to me?"

"Your face has fallen victim to the tragedies of non-waterproof mascara, Jess. Here, use this," says Chloe, handing me a wipe from her backpack.

I wipe my face until the black paint, or as Chloe calls it, "mascara," is gone. I'm confused as to what it was, but I don't ask.

Of the many questions I have about this place called high school and this girl I'm now disguised as, this doesn't seem like an important one.

"I'll re-apply your mascara," says Chloe, taking out a pink tube. She hands me a brush. "You might want to sort out your hair."

As I brush my hair, which refuses to be as smooth as it was before, Chloe opens the pink tube to reveal what looks like a wand. She runs it over my eyelashes, leaving them longer and more noticeable, just like they were before. Looking in the mirror, my reflection is very different to what the sixteen-year-old me looked like when I first met her this morning. But with a few more minutes of work, Chloe has me closer to my sixteen-year-old self. The girl I barely know.

"That's better," she says, helping me brush out one last knot. "Let's get back to class now."

"What about my birthmark? We need to make it go away again like my big kid— like *I* want... yes, that's it! *I* hate it. It's ugly."

Chloe stares at me, and for a second, I think I see tears in her eyes.

"I don't have any concealer, Jess, I'm sorry. But please trust me — your birthmark is cute! It looks like a giraffe. In a good way."

I stare at my older self's reflection in the mirror, and for a second, I think I see tears in her eyes. My eyes. Our eyes.

"Jess? We should head back to class."

As soon as we return, the big kids stare at us again, and I decide if I'm going to stay in this school, I better get used to that.

Rye leads me back to our table.

"Are you okay, Jess?"

"Is lunch soon?"

"Ten minutes."

"Then yes."

Looking into his eyes, I see the faint glow of his kindergarten years, but when I blink, it goes away.

When I look at the lab in front of me, I feel like an idiot. An idiot for wanting to switch into being a big kid, an idiot for not understanding almost anything so far today; I feel like an idiot for cheating my years. But at least lunch is easy to understand. It seems like lunch will be the first part of being a big kid that doesn't make me feel stupid.

6

16 years of youth

I am so smart.

Being surrounded by kindergarteners really boosts my self-confidence, even though I know I have an unfair intellectual advantage. But nonetheless, I'm ecstatic. I no longer feel like a complete failure. If I never switch back, will I eventually get so much smarter than everyone else I'll become one of those kids who goes to college at age twelve? Maybe Albert Einstein wasn't a genius at birth, but someone who switched his years from youth to younger, giving him a constant lead over everyone else. Someday, my name might be in those fancy textbooks. Kids will learn about me and wonder how I got to be such a brilliant intellect. I can picture them saying that nobody will ever be as smart as Jessica Locke. They'll call me a genius, and they'll strive to be like me. Any teacher who ever had the audacity to give me a B would immediately be fired.

It would be great. But it wouldn't be real.

At many points today, I've found myself thinking, am I actually smart? To which I answer, yes, Jess, you know ten times as much as any other student here. But now I remember: at the end of the day, I'll have to switch back to my sixteen-year-old self, because, "*only at*

73

school will you switch your years / this should protect you from at-home tears." But that's simply not true. Being back in my natural years will be far more stressful. I want to stay young forever, but there's no way of escaping it. I'll just have to do everything in my power to stay in kindergarten as long as possible.

"Who's excited to learn?" asks Mrs. Rose.

Although I won't be gaining any previously unknown academic knowledge, I'll sure learn something. Maybe even more than these kindergarteners will.

The little kids, along with the out of place high schooler, sit in a circle around Mrs. Rose. She sets up colorful, connectable cubes on a small table, then looks at us and smiles. I can't help but smile back.

"We're now going to be learning about simple addition and subtraction," she says. "Who would like to tell me what those mean?"

I raise my hand.

"Addition is the action of increasing the number of something, and subtraction is the action of decreasing the number of something."

"Very good, Jessica! You're on a roll today," she says, handing me a sticker.

I'm sure I would be more content if the compliment was for my true years. But my false youth doesn't smile at deception.

"Let's start with subtraction. If I have these sixteen cubes and take away these ten cubes, how many do I have left?"

She waits. Aimee and I are the only ones to raise our hands, and Mrs. Rose calls on her.

"You have six."

"Good job, Aimee," she says, but she doesn't seem as impressed as she did with my wits. "Now let's try addition. If I have these ten cubes and add six, how many do I have?"

She adds cubes one by one, and this time, I'm the only one who seems to know.

"I need to see more hands, or else I'll have to pick from the cup of names."

Three kindergarteners raise their hands, most likely just trying to avoid having their names picked involuntarily. When I think about it, I realize it's kind of like TAYFABYAPA, except I'm here in kindergarten instead of high school. It's basically the same thing, except the names are picked randomly instead of by who looks the least engaged in class, and it doesn't seem to have multiple stages of embarrassment. But other than that, it's the same. Or maybe the only similarities come from me hopelessly searching for any hidden traces of my real years.

Mrs. Rose looks around the circle and calls on Chloe.

"You have sixteen."

"Excellent! Now, if I subtract eleven cubes from the sixteen I already have, how many will I have then?"

The kindergarteners stare at her in silence, as if anticipating something.

"I'm not going to move them this time. You'll just have to imagine it, so it's going to be tricky."

I raise my hand, alone in doing so. Seeing I volunteered, Aimee does the same.

"What is your answer, Aimee?"

"Four," she says with that familiar, *I-am-so-much-better-than-everyone* expression she seems to always have plastered on her face in high school.

"Close, but not quite. Jessica?"

"Five."

"Great job!" says Mrs. Rose. Aimee looks mortified.

We spend the rest of learning time going over material so simple I think I learned it in preschool. It goes the same way all class: I'm the only one to raise my hand, so Mrs. Rose threatens to pull names from the cup of popsicle sticks, then more kindergarteners volunteer. Everyone looks at me as though I'm a genius, and I absolutely love it. "How are you so smart, Jess?" they ask. "How can I become as smart as you?" Oh, if only they knew. I'm at the top of my class, and right now, I feel like I'm on top of the world.

But if you put a squirrel next to a pile of rocks, does that make it clever?

6 years of youth

I feel like I'm trapped in a school filled with Albert Einsteins. And I'm the only one who doesn't know anything.

I feel like someone took my brain and left me with only a tiny piece. Or maybe someone took my true years, and left me with only the mask of way too many.

I feel like the only person to blame is me.

Right now, it's lunchtime — a well-deserved break, if I do say so my six-year-old self. I follow Rye into a huge room filled with neatly organized tables, chairs, and a few large trash cans. Unlike kindergarten, the walls have no posters and are painted in only dull colors. The room is much more packed than the lunchroom in kindergarten, but there's a somewhat neat, almost single-file line at the front of the room. Even though everyone brings lunch from home in kindergarten, it's the closest reminder of my real years.

I want to stand in line with them, because I'm sure I'd be good at it. I'd impress all the big kids with my line-standing skills! But when I look at Rye, I know the real big kid me would spend all her time at lunch with him.

And I've been copying her all day.

"Wanna sit outside today, Jess?" he asks.

"Are we allowed to?" I ask, avoiding his eyes. There's no way big kids get *that* many privileges. They already get to run in the halls and yell in class without getting a time-out.

"Of course we are!" he says, laughing a little. "We sat outside yesterday, remember?"

No. I don't remember. Yesterday, my years were real. Rye will just have to deal with how stupid I am.

"Yes, of course I remember!" I say. "I love sitting outside! Sitting outside is the *best!* One question: can we see the kindergarten if we eat lunch outside? I mean... I don't care. Not at all. I just forgot."

"No, the kindergarten's on the other side of the building," says Rye. I look into his eyes for just a second, and when I do, I see concern. So I try to fix it.

"I was just joking! I already knew that."

I follow his lead outside through a set of double doors. There's a few small tables here, and I sit across from Rye, picking at the chipped wood. Only a few other big kids are outside, so it's much quieter, and the sun shines so bright I have to squint to see clearly. My eyes still burn a little, but I know it's not from the sun. I'm too embarrassed from last class to be excited about getting to eat outside, and I'm too confused by my years to focus on the light.

"Was the class laughing at me?" I ask, even though I already know the answer.

"Yes. But who cares about them? I know you've had a rough day, Jess, but you always get through it."

"Today's been rough, alright."

I look at the ground, feeling sadness once again. When I look back at him, his eyes are still focused on mine.

"You know you can always talk to me."

But I can't talk to him. Not really. I guess I could say, "Surprise! I'm the kindergarten version of Jess! That's why today's been rough." But I remember what I was told: *"do not tell others about your youth's tricks / or you will have problems you cannot fix."*

So my years stay silent.

I look into my big kid backpack and find a lunchbox with a complicated black and white pattern. Inside is a turkey and cheese sandwich, chips, fruit, and a chocolate bar. Rye takes out a lunchbox too, and together, we eat and talk about whatever it is a high schooler and a kindergartener are supposed to talk about. Maybe to him, everything seems normal.

"Tomorrow should be better," he says. "I'm excited for Valentine's Day."

I think that's the holiday when, being the big kid I now am, I'm supposed to get chocolate and flowers.

"I think I am too," I say. Then, remembering my manners, I ask, "What do you want for a gift?"

I know it's not my job to get him anything, but I'm curious. Maybe I could even help the sixteen-year-old me.

"Whatever you get me," he says. "Even if it's nothing at all."

"Okey-dokey, artichokey," I say, even though I'm still not sure if big kids are supposed to.

Probably not.

When I smile, Rye does the same.

"Do you remember the first time we talked?"

"Yes. It was after you fell off the monkey bars in kindergarten," I say, thinking back to earlier today, before the switch. And then I realize: after the switch, the day started over, which means that, in some weird way, learning time and recess never actually happened. But at the same time, I know they did. They had to have.

"You smell like gingerbread cookies."

"Or maybe that's just this gingerbread cookie," he says, taking one out of his lunchbox. "Do you want half? My mom made it."

I gladly accept. He splits the cookie in two and gives me the bigger piece.

"Are you excited for gym class?"

That must be the "physical education" on my schedule. Even though I hate exercise, I don't think it can be too bad.

"Are you gonna be there?"

"I will."

"Then yes."

We talk until lunch is over, and I think I'm future in love.

16 years of youth

I think I'm in love.

I'm in love with my newfound lack of stress, in love with being at the top of my class. I'm in love with sitting on the ground in a circle instead of at an uncomfortable desk, and I'm profoundly in love with the cuteness factor of six-year-old Rye. I'm in love with kindergarten. But I hate the feeling of my years being fragile and fake.

"Lunchtime!" yells Mrs. Rose, and all the little kids cheer. I grab my bright pink lunchbox from my butterfly-patterned backpack, but Mrs. Rose stops us before we can line up at the door.

"Wait!" she says. "I have a challenge for you. Today at lunch, you are going to get the chance to talk to someone new!"

Laura and Mindi look annoyed, Aimee looks intrigued, and Rye looks confused. Chloe looks at me and frowns, probably because, from what little I can remember from kindergarten, we always sat together at lunch. And I don't know what to feel. This is my first day here in ten years.

"I'm going to pull pairs of names from the cup, and that will be who you will sit with at lunch today. Sound good?"

Most of the kids whine, as immature kindergarteners do. Mrs. Rose ignores them.

This might be the first part of kindergarten that actually manages to make me stressed. Being forced to spend a whole lunch talking with six-year-old Laura or Mindi sounds miserable. Knowing them, they'll probably find something new to make fun of me about.

"Hey, Jessica, your sandwich is cut unevenly and looks stupid, just like your face!" they might say. Or, *"Hey, Jessica, those polka-dot pants were* so *two weeks ago!"*

Whatever they say, I don't think there's a good chance of it being nice. The insults would be meant for my other years, but they're still a part of my sixteen. And yes, I'm a teenage girl who's dreading the possibility of having to sit next to kindergarten bullies. Anything that involves interacting outside my small bubble of acceptable people has always been an anxiety trigger for me. I don't think time could ever change that.

"Are you ready to see who you'll be sitting with?"

Mrs. Rose picks the first two names.

"First pair is Laura and Mindi."

That solves that problem. Laura cheers obnoxiously, but Mindi seems disappointed. I would be too if I were her.

"Second pair is Chloe and Aimee."

Chloe looks at Aimee with a friendly smile, but Aimee's expression remains unchanged. This is probably because, "Unnecessary smiling triggers the brain into a state of disingenuous contentment, rendering the action immensely illogical," as she says in high school.

High school...

"Next pair is Rye and Jessica."

Rye and I look at each other and smile, and with my false youth and his true years, I feel younger. We often eat lunch together in high school, so despite the new reality of this being Rye from ten years ago, and the bending rules of age, this shouldn't be too much different for him. But I'm sure it will be different for me.

Mrs. Rose pairs the rest of the kids, then we line up at the door in a neat, single-file line. The kindergarteners follow her lead through the nearly empty, quiet hallways, and an out of place high schooler tags behind.

Not far from our classroom is a slightly larger room filled with tables and a few more groups of five and six-year-olds, and as we walk inside, my memory reignites. The room is plastered with posters displaying personified fruits, vegetables, and other foods with happy faces. Where there are no animated foods, the walls are covered in bright paint of all colors with no pattern or limits. The random blobs and streaks appear so unorganized, you would think they were designed by a kindergartener, somehow making the atmosphere even more familiar and comforting. I sit at a small, bright blue table in the middle of the room, and Rye sits across from me. We take out our lunches and immediately engage in conversation.

"You know, I'm glad we get to sit together," he says. "I'd rather talk to you for five hours than talk to one of *those* girls for five minutes."

He points to Laura and Mindi, who sit at a table a few feet away from us.

"Thanks! If I had to choose between a luxury box of chocolates or talking with you, I would definitely talk with you."

"Really? I must be pretty interesting," he says, blushing. "What do you have for lunch today?"

I look into my six-year-old self's lunchbox, which is much smaller and brighter than my own.

"I have a peanut butter and jelly sandwich, chips, fruit, and a chocolate bar," I say, realizing it's not that much different from what

I normally bring to high school. But right now, I don't want to be reminded of my real years.

We eat in silence for a few minutes, a silence that probably would have been awkward if it wasn't Rye I was with. Then I decide to make conversation. I am the "big kid" here, after all.

"What's your favorite color?"

"Rainbow," he replies instantly. "I think if I chose only one color, it would hurt the others' feelings. I know they're not alive, so they don't actually have feelings... but I like to pretend. What's yours?"

"I don't have one," I say. "So I guess mine is rainbow, too."

"You remind me of blue cheese."

"Thanks. How so?"

"Because you're special. You're not like regular cheese."

"Well, what's different?" I ask, even though I understand perfectly.

"You see, most cheese is only yellow, but blue cheese is brave enough to have parts of it be blue. I mean, you're not *really* cheese, but—"

"I know exactly what you mean," I say. "You remind me of chocolate."

"Why?"

"Because you're awesome," I say, realizing six-year-old Rye is better at making analogies than I am.

"Thanks! I found a cool rock outside yesterday, and I think I'm gonna name it after you. It's in a jar in my room now," he says, his eyes lighting up with the youth mine lack. "What was that 'Ryjess' thing you were telling me about at recess? You said you would tell me later, and I'm not so sure, but I think it's 'later' now."

Pausing for a moment, I think about sixteen-year-old Rye. I think about how he's different from his kindergarten self, and how he's similar. I think about our real years, and my age-deceptive wish. I think of this in the span of a few rushed seconds, then I stop. And I live in the moment.

A moment that shouldn't exist.

"'Ryjess' is a combination of our names. 'Ry' is for Rye, and 'Jess' is for Jessica. I used our combined names to form the word 'out*ryjess*.' It's 'outrageous,' but with an added touch of Rye and Jess."

He stares at me with a look of wonder.

"So we have our own word?"

"We do," I say. "And that makes me out*ryjess*ly happy."

He raises an eyebrow.

"I have a question," he says. "What does 'outrageous' mean?"

Oh, right. This is kindergarten. Kindergarten kids, kindergarten classes. Kindergarten vocabulary.

"That's a word you won't need to know until you're a big kid," I say. "I only know it because a big kid told me."

He still seems confused, but he's smiling nonetheless. His smile stays until we hear a voice from the table next to us call—

"Hey, *Jessica!*"

We both turn toward Laura and Mindi.

"Jessica, do you have any candy?" asks Mindi, staring at the ground. "If you have some you don't want, we could trade, or—"

"Mindi!" snaps Laura. She looks at me and speaks twice as loud as Mindi. "Jessica, do you have any candy?"

"Yes."

She looks at Mindi with a smile of false victory.

"You better give up your candy, Jessica, or else we'll start crying and tell Mrs. Rose it's because of how ugly you are! You'll be in *so* much trouble!"

They sit quietly and wait for me to respond. If only they knew about my years.

"Alright, then," I say. "I'll give up my candy."

I take the chocolate bar out of my lunchbox and hand it to Rye. The looks on Laura and Mindi's faces fill me with childish glee.

"Thanks!" says Rye. "Do you want this gingerbread cookie now?"

"I would be delighted," I say. And we eat dessert.

6 years of youth

"I would be delighted," I say in my land of daydreams.

In my imagination, I respond to Rye asking me to marry him, sort of like how it goes in all my favorite fairy tales. As we walk back into the school, I find myself imagining an impossible future, even though I know it's silly. Maybe my next wish should be to switch to a time when Rye and I are happily married, living in a castle far away. We would both live forever, because nothing could ever take our years away.

But I don't believe in magic; I don't believe in Santa, the Tooth Fairy, the Easter Bunny. Not anymore.

We walk through the packed hallways toward a room called "athletic center" where we both have to be next. I have no idea where to find it, so I just follow Rye. It's a lot more fun than following Mrs. Rose in kindergarten, for sure. As we walk, I think about what he might say if I told him who I am. Yes, I'm still Jessica Jule Locke, but I'm not the me he thinks I am. If I told him my mind is six years old, would he even believe me? I know I can't tell him, but I'm curious.

I have so many questions. From only talking with the big kid me for a few minutes, I don't know much about her. Am I a lot smarter as a big kid? Am I cooler, funnier, and just overall better than I am now? Does age make one better? If I were to switch with my eighty-year-old self, would I find her life to be better than all the years I've lived? I know it would be different, but I can't decide whether different would be good or bad. Of all the six years I've lived so far, I know that being six has been better than being five or four. But I still don't think I know enough about my sixteen-year-old self's life to know if her years make her happier. When I saw her this morning, as her true self, she didn't seem as glad to be a big kid as I thought she would be. She must have been pretty sad, or else she wouldn't have made the wish to switch.

So what are the rules of age?

Rye and I walk into a big, almost empty room with the highest ceiling of all the classes I've seen so far. There's only a few other big kids around, and a woman with a friendly face approaches us.

"Your teacher isn't here today, so I'll be your substitute. We're going to meet in the auditorium to watch a video on the importance of daily exercise and a well-balanced diet."

Two substitutes in one day? Mrs. Rose is only ever absent once every few months! A video on diet and exercise doesn't sound interesting at all, but I'm sure it will be better than learning about triangles. I'm sure my sixteen-year-old self wishes she could be here. But she can't.

Rye leads the way to a room unlike any of the others I've seen today. It looks kind of like a movie theatre, except the front of the room is higher up than the rest, and there's a big, thin screen that looks like a strange piece of paper. There's probably thousands— maybe millions!— of seats, but only the first couple of rows are filled. Rye and I sit three rows from the front.

The woman we saw in the last room now stands in front of the screen, looking around as if searching for someone. After a few seconds, she turns toward us and smiles.

"I know we're supposed to watch a video on the importance of daily exercise and a well-balanced diet, but that's no fun. So I thought I'd play an animated movie instead!"

The big kids cheer, and I join them. This will be the second movie I watch in high school today! I guess I chose the right day to come. And the sixteen-year-old me chose the wrong day to leave.

The woman sets up the movie on the screen, and the room gets louder as all the big kids talk about whatever it is big kids talk about. And the kindergartener listens.

"You know," says Rye, "a lot about you hasn't changed much since we were younger."

Oh, no. I think he's onto me. What if he knows about the switch and is testing me to see if I'll say anything? What if he hates that I switched my years, and wants the sixteen-year-old me back? What if —

"You have the same smile, the same humor, the same personality — the same perfection," he says. "The best parts about you haven't changed a bit."

My mask of years is a trick. And he's falling for it.

"Thanks," I say. "You have a nice face."

Looking into his eyes, I see the faint glow of his kindergarten years, but when I blink, it goes away.

The lights go down, the movie plays, and even though my years are old, I feel so young.

16 years of youth

I feel so old.

Talking with six-year-old Rye in a place I haven't seen in ten years brings out a feeling much stronger than nostalgia. Until today, kindergarten was a memory so distant I could barely grasp it. Now, it feels strangely familiar.

Lunch is over, and we're back in the classroom where Mrs. Rose sets up various toys and games for active play. To me, it seems like just another recess, but I know the main point of it is to teach the valuable life lesson of "sharing is caring." For a multitude of reasons, I already know this skill by heart. I share my years with a kindergartener. And I steal my youth from what sets us apart.

"Time for active play!" says Mrs. Rose. "As usual, use your inside voices, share with others, and make sure no one is playing alone. Agree?"

"Agree!" yells the class of five and six-year-olds. The high schooler stays silent.

Most of the kids move toward the board games, so I sit on a rug with building blocks. Immediately, Rye and Chloe both sit next to me.

"No!" says Chloe to Rye. "Jess is *my* friend!"

Rye gives her a shy smile.

"She's my friend too."

"But I've known her longer! And Jess and I have friendship bracelets. Do *you* and Jess have friendship bracelets, Rye? *Huh?* I didn't think—"

"You can both be my friends," I say. The differences between their kindergarten and high school years become clearer every minute I stay here.

"Don't worry, Chloe, I'm a nice person," says Rye.

Chloe glares at him fixedly.

"Are you two dating?"

"No," Rye and I say simultaneously.

"We're only in kindergarten," I add, trying to constantly remind myself of this new fact. "Maybe someday, when we're big kids, we will."

Maybe. A disheartening cross between yes and no that almost always seems to land on the negative. But my years already know. And the answer is a blaring yes.

Chloe narrows her eyes at Rye, then turns back to me.

"Jess, are you sure we shouldn't just forget he's in our class?" she whispers in my ear. Rye frowns, and I shake my head at Chloe. I am the big kid here, after all.

Chloe crosses her arms.

"Fine, Rye!" she says. "I guess you're not *horrible*. We can both be friends with Jess."

"Thanks, I guess," says Rye. He looks at the blocks on the rug, then his smile returns. "We should build these into a giant tower!"

"We could make it reach the ceiling!" says Chloe.

The imagination of kindergarteners is like nothing I'll ever experience again. It's crazy that my six-year-old self thought to grow up in such an untraditional way. And it's crazy I let my youth wander.

The three of us slowly build a tower, taking turns adding one block at a time with exceptional precision. Once it's six blocks high, Aimee sits next to us.

"It will fall if you add another block," she says.

I add another block, and sure enough, our tower falls. How can someone be so smart in kindergarten? You know, other than using the unique method of having sixteen years in a six-year-old's body.

"You need to build it on the tiles, not the rug," says Aimee. "The unevenness of the rug makes the tower less sturdy."

Taking her advice, the four of us start a new tower on the floor tiles. We build up to sixteen blocks, then stop to admire our creation.

"I've never built it this high before," says Chloe. "This is so cool!"

"I think so, too," says Rye. "If you use your imagination, it almost reaches the ceiling."

From across the room, Laura and Mindi slowly walk toward us, seemingly intrigued by our excellent tower. The three kindergarteners next to me barely seem to notice their presence, but I immediately sense trouble.

"Cool tower you got there!" says Laura. "It would be a shame if — *oops!*"

She knocks over our tower with her foot, and Mindi looks at her with what seems to be genuine surprise. Laura wears a proud smile as Chloe, Rye, and Aimee take on frowns. Of all the children in this room, Laura is undoubtedly the most childish.

"I'm *so* sorry, it was an *accident!*" she says, throwing her hands into the air. Mindi peers around the room with wide eyes, but Laura doesn't seem remotely concerned. To my gratitude, Mrs. Rose walks over, and Laura's perfect little grin evaporates.

"I am very disappointed in you, Laura," she says. "I'm going to have to report this to your parents."

"But... no! I... *WAHHH!*"

She pretends to cry, but it's not convincing in the slightest.

"That's not going to work this time," says Mrs. Rose. "Don't expect any stickers any time soon."

Laura scowls at us, and Mindi slowly walks away.

"As for you, Jessica, Rye, Chloe, and Aimee— you will all get stickers for how well you handled Laura's unacceptable behavior."

We give each other high fives, and I relish the joy of seeing Laura in trouble, even though this is only kindergarten.

One block at a time, we rebuild our tower. Before active play is over, we build it back up to sixteen. When it's time to clean up, my years feel even falser, but the joy of being young is so true. With permission from the kindergarteners, I knock over the tower and clean up the pieces.

If my youth is on my side, I could get used to this.

6 years of youth

I could get used to this.

Here in high school, we watch movies and get more time to eat lunch. Here in high school, Rye likes me and has talked to me more so far today than he ever has in kindergarten. Here in high school, classes are hard, but I don't mind.

There in kindergarten, everything's different.

There in kindergarten, I get playtime, recess, and lessons I actually understand. There in kindergarten, I'm with my years. There in kindergarten, I'm me. But here in high school, I'm the me I would rather be.

I could get used to this. But my years could never do the same.

It's the end of the day and just about time for me to go back to my real years. But I don't know how to feel. Being older is what I wanted, after all. It was my wish to switch just as much as it was my sixteen-year-old self's. My mother once told me to be careful what I wish for.

After I make it through the mobs of big kids in the hallways, I run to the grass between the kindergarten and high school building, then I sit and wait. I'm tired from my long day of work and lack of play, but I still don't know if I want to return. My brain is packed with so many thoughts I couldn't possibly think them all. Kindergarten is never this complicated. And kindergarten is never this interesting.

After a few moments of thinking, my locket buzzes. I open it and unfold a piece of paper that reads aloud:

it is the end of your first day of the switch, and you have done well / your sixteen years of youth will meet you here, but of your experiences you must not tell / you will switch lockets, which will switch back your years / you must be your true self when not at school, even if it brings fears / you will see your sixteen years of youth in your body, but don't be alarmed / no one else will be able to see you, and this experiment will not be harmed / soon you will go, but you won't be left behind / you will simply return to your sixteen years of youth's mind

Well, that makes no sense. None of this does. I've learned by now that age is confusing. And time doesn't follow the rules of age.

I look up to see who I know to be Jessica Jule Locke staring at me, but with my sixteen-year-old self's mind.

Without saying a word, we switch lockets, and the ground spins. After the spinning stops, I'm back as my kindergarten self.

Being a kindergartener in high school just doesn't make sense anymore. I want to be me. My mind, my body, my years— all mine.

I walk toward my sixteen years of youth, but she backs away. Big kid Jess gives me a smile, yet her eyes show sadness. And I know we can't stay here together.

My years walk away.

7

16 years of youth

At some points today, I've missed being the real me.

I've missed talking with high school Rye and Chloe. I've missed having privileges I just don't have in kindergarten. And believe it or not, I've missed the challenges that come with high school. Re-learning information I've known for ten years has become tedious. My brain feels dehydrated from lack of new knowledge, yet my mind is floating in an ocean of curiosity— curiosity as to what staying in kindergarten will bring, curiosity as to how different things will feel when I'm back home with my years. Even though I'm required to be in my true years at home, will I still feel younger from a school day of youth?

I love it here in kindergarten. But I learn more there in high school. I want to stay here in kindergarten as long as my years will allow. But I belong there in high school. My years are lost, hopelessly indecisive. But being young is what youth is all about.

So when I saw her standing outside the neighboring, yet ever so distant buildings, my worries evaporated. I was relieved to walk away and feel my years follow me.

My years on my mind, I sit one row from the front of my bus home. Not yet used to being back in my own body, I run my hands through the hair I straightened before curling lightly this morning.

Strangely, it's not as smooth as usual, but that could just be my imagination. After a day of my kindergarten self's frizzy, out of control hair, my own is bound to feel different. Many of my features appear to be amiss. My white, flower-patterned shirt has a bright yellow stain, and my eyes burn noticeably, yet not overpoweringly. My six-year-old self could have just cried a lot today. She could have felt her false years as a burning fire. Or maybe I'm just imagining it.

Moving all the way to the end of the seat, I look out the window and stare at all the high schoolers walking to their busses. It feels as though it's been ages since I've seen them. I bet they'd be jealous if they knew I got to spend the day in kindergarten. But I do wonder if there's anything I've missed today.

"Hey, crybaby!" I look over to see Laura and Mindi sitting in the seat across from me. Mindi stares peacefully out the window until her troublesome companion nudges her.

"*Wahhh!*" says Laura, horribly imitating a cry. "I *bit my tongue.*"

She laughs, but Mindi stays silent.

"I have no idea what you're talking about."

"Don't you remember English class, Jessica?"

No. No, I don't. I want to tell them, but I can't. My wish is a furtive whisper, and my false years are a thundering scream. Imagining my six-year-old self's day in high school makes me cringe. She surely made a fool of herself. Made a fool of me.

"You don't wanna talk about it, Jessica? Why, did Rye tell you not to talk to us?" asks Laura. "Did your *strong and mighty* boyfriend tell you to ignore us?"

Oh, no. *Rye.* My kindergarten self's conversations with him must have been interesting. Or horrifying. Probably both.

"No, but that sounds like a swell idea to me," I say, putting in headphones to listen to music. The bus moves, my music plays, and I'm me again.

***

I open my front door, toss my backpack on the ground, and collapse onto the couch in my living room. Home, sweet home. Kindergarten was nice. But nothing is better than home.

Just as I'm about to relax, I remember that, despite my absence in high school today, I'm still bound to have homework. And I doubt my kindergarten self wrote it down in my agenda for me. So I text Chloe.

Jess: *Hey, what's the homework? I totally forgot to write it down.*

She responds within a minute.

Chloe: *Worksheet for math, reading questions for English, and you have to finish the lab worksheet for chemistry by Friday. Are you okay?*

Jess: *Yeah, why?*

Oh, how I know.

Chloe: *You haven't been acting like yourself today.*

I've been acting like myself, but in my wrong years.

Jess: *I'm fine.*

Kind of.

Chloe: *Is all the sulfur out of your eyes yet?*

Sulfur in my eyes? That would explain the burning, but I can think of no conceivable explanation as to how it got there. I don't want to imagine it.

Jess: *Everything's fine. I gotta go do homework now. I'll see you tomorrow.*

I turn off my phone, open my backpack, and prepare to face the harsh reality of high school again. At least I didn't have to do all the work I would have otherwise had to in class. That was a problem for six-year-old Jess.

Although my six years of youth is now simply a creature of my mind, where she belongs, I can't help but wonder what she would be thinking right now if this was ten years ago and she was in this house as a kindergartener. A different world, a different time. Same Jessica.

6 years of youth

As soon as I get home, I know something is strange.

Here I am in my house just as it was before the switch, but somehow, I know my older years are here too. The locket's message that I will return to my older self's mind confuses me. I don't know if I believe it, but maybe that's where I am right now. My years are capable of anything. Everything feels different, yet everything looks the same. Same world, same time. Different Jessica.

I rush into my living room, eager to enjoy being home again. My six-month-old twin brothers, Jacob and Jerry, are crying so loudly I cover my ears, and my mom looks as stressed as I was when I first realized the challenges of being a big kid. Some dumb show I'm far too old to watch is playing on TV, but my brothers seem uninterested.

"Mom, can I change the channel?"

She jumps a little and looks at me, seemingly forgetting I was home.

"No, Jess, wait until I calm down your brothers."

"But why?"

She doesn't respond, instead running into the kitchen to get food for the twins.

"Mom?"

She stays silent.

I think my brothers are too young to have problems, but my mom says they constantly wail because that's just how babies are. Another rule of age. After being fed, the cries slowly stop, and my mom turns toward me.

"Jess, could you please hand me the toy box?"

I roll my eyes and reach for a box filled with the most pointless toys. My mom smiles, but her eyes look tired. Before Jacob and Jerry existed, everything was calm and quiet. My parents spent every second focused on me, and I almost always got to decide what to watch on TV. Whenever I got upset, they would calm me down and play games with me until everything was okay. Now, if I cry, they say I'm too old to be acting up, and I have to listen to my brothers fuss without complaining. When the twins are older, I know it will be different. Some day, they'll be too old for crying. By then, I'll be much older too, without my years being fake.

Age changes everything. But age is so slow.

"Mom, can we—"

"*WAHHH!*"

My mom cradles my crying brothers, and I want to weep with them. But I'm far too mature for that. I'm not an ordinary kindergartener anymore, and even though I can't tell anyone about my day in high school, I can show that I won't accept being ignored.

"Mom?"

No response.

"Mom!"

Nothing.

"*Mom!*"

The louder my voice gets, the louder the babies cry. My mom freezes. When my voice stops, she continues comforting my brothers.

"Keep your voice down, Jessica! You know better," she says, her eyes still glued to the twins. "What were you going to say?"

"Can we play a game?"

I don't look into her eyes, because I know they will show how annoyed she is. Before she speaks, I know the answer.

"Not now, Jess, I'm sorry," she says, finally meeting my eyes. "I have to take care of your brothers."

I stomp my foot and rush upstairs. The young ones continue their tears as the old sister hates her years. I close my door quietly, even though I want to slam it. Then I sit on my bed and try to ignore the crazy world around me. And I think about tomorrow. Alone.

***

Never in all my days of my six years have I been more excited to sleep. I'm far too tired to stay up late, so going to bed early and forgetting about my worries should be extra rewarding after all the confusion from my wish. Today, it's a good reminder I'm not sixteen. I'm six.

At school, my years are free to be false, but at home, they have to be true. I don't think that will ever change. So after my family and I eat dinner, I complain about my long, tiring day at school, without the details, of course. I'm not *that* stupid.

I walk up to my pink-walled room with its dolls and coloring supplies on the floor everywhere. My big kid self's room must look totally different. She must have makeup, textbooks, and no dolls, because those are only for little kids. I know it's the same space, but because her years are so different, I know our rooms look nothing alike. I must have changed a lot with time.

After a few minutes of sitting on my bed and looking around my room as if I've never seen it before, I try to fall asleep and forget about my problems. You know, the ones that come as a part of going to high school as a kindergartener? The ones that arrived as soon as I switched into my false years? Those. I never thought I would have to deal with those problems, but at least high school isn't quite as bad as the stories I've heard. And I never thought I would get to experience it so soon.

As I slowly fall asleep, the sixteen-year-old me is probably doing all of the homework I got today. It's strange to think that somewhere, somehow, she's in this same house, but with ten more years, I know nothing will be the same. Right now, she's nowhere to be found, and no trace of high school has followed me here. Well, maybe a certain big kid has been on my mind...

Rye. I almost forgot about him. If I had another wish today, it would be to have the Rye I know talk to me as much in kindergarten as he talks to the big kid me. Maybe if I wish long enough, he'll appear at my door with a flower. Or maybe that's only a high school thing.

Instead of thinking any longer, I decide to count on my dreams. I close my eyes and see a storm of colors.

16 years of youth

Ding, dong.

I put away my completed homework. From the window, I see Rye. Oh, how I've missed him. He holds something in his hands, but from where I stand, I have no clue what it could be. I hastily open the door.

"I got you this artichoke," he says, lo and behold, with an artichoke.

"Um... *thanks*! What's the occasion?"

"Well, I was just thinking about how cute it was today when you said 'okey-dokey artichokey.' So I went to the store, and now I'm here at your door with this artichoke."

My youth smiles. That phrase was one I said quite often when I was six. Maybe I'll start using it again. Or maybe I should let her years belong solely to her, and my years belong solely to me. But after today, I know it's not that simple. And I'm glad.

"That is the most romantic thing I've ever heard."

"Also, my mom drove me here and said she'll drive us to Starbucks. Wanna come?"

"That is the second most romantic thing I've ever heard."

I grab my phone, my purse, and my years, then head out the door and outside with Rye. His mom's car is parked in my driveway, and we sit next to each other in the two back seats.

"Hello, Jessica!" says Mrs. Arthur. "Rye, sweetie, did you give her the artichoke? I thought that was such a cute idea!"

"Yes, Mom," says Rye, blushing.

"I also thought it was a cute idea," I add.

"Oh, yes, so cute. You see, when Rye here asked me to take him to the supermarket to get an artichoke, I downright thought he had lost his marbles! But it turns out it was just a romantic gesture, a mighty thoughtful one at that. Rye, when would you like me to drive you to that store to get the— *oops!* I can't give away the surprise, now, can I? Sorry, Rye; sorry, Jessica."

"*Mom*," says Rye, "saying there's a surprise is giving away a part of the surprise."

"Oh, right. Just kidding, Jessica! No surprise."

"Mom!"

"It's fine," I say, laughing. "I'll just pretend I didn't hear a thing."

"Good," says Mrs. Arthur. "I wouldn't want to give away the surprise."

"How about you turn on the radio, Mom?" asks Rye, his face turning red.

"I think we should just talk," I say. "It'll be like a mini Starbucks road trip adventure."

Rye looks at me as though I just said something crazy. But to me, the definition of "crazy" will never be the same.

"So, Mrs. Arthur, how's your day going?" I ask.

"It's going mighty grand! My favorite song was on the radio this morning, I got double pink Starbursts in my pack of two I had for a snack, and here I am with my son and his lovely girlfriend," she says. "How are you, dear?"

"I'm doing pretty swell," I say. "Thank you for driving us."

"It's no problem at all," she says. "Jessica, since you kids are going to Starbucks, this is the perfect time for me to ask you: what are your opinions on iced coffee?"

"I think it's alright," I say. "What about you?"

"I think it's wonderful! You see, coffee beans need lots of water to grow. So when frozen cubes of water are added to coffee, the substance that brought it to life joins it in the form of a delectable drink. And I think that's amazing."

"I never thought about it that way," I say. "This totally changes my perspective on iced coffee."

"It changed my perspective too. I've also never seen pickles the same way until I sat down and *really* thought about it. You see..."

We discuss the deep, ambiguous meaning behind various food items for the rest of the car ride. And dealing with such ambiguity, I can't help but think of my years, both false and true. But right now, all I want is to be me. My mind, my body, my years— all mine.

We pull into the Starbucks parking lot, and my years feel alive and free.

"Alright, you two, here we are," says Mrs. Arthur. "Rye, do you need money or do you have your own?"

"I brought my own," he says. "I'm not a kid anymore, Mom."

"Okay, dear, I was just checking," she says. "Call me when you need a ride home."

Rye and I step out of the car. Mrs. Arthur waves, and we walk toward our favorite coffee shop's entrance.

"Your mom's cool," I say. Maybe it's because of her years.

"Yeah, she's great," says Rye. "Except, sometimes she treats me like I'm as young as Dustin. I feel like she tends to forget I'm so much older than he is."

He refers to his six-year-old brother, who has always struck me as one of the happiest kids I know. He reminds me a lot of kindergarten Rye.

"Age is confusing," I say, speaking from experience. Far too much experience.

Rye and I sit at a booth next to a large, half-open window. Unlike this morning, my six years of youth is nowhere on the other side of the glass.

Rye stands and looks at me with sixteen years.

"What can I get for you today?"

"I brought money," I say. "I can pay."

"No, I got it. Think of it as an *I'm-Sorry-You-Got-Sulfur-In-Your-Eyes* treat."

I still have no idea how the "sulfur in my eyes" incident occurred, but I just smile and try not to think about my kindergarten self in high school.

"I'll have an iced coffee with espresso, please."

"And?" he asks, knowing I have a sweet tooth.

"Whatever type of cake pop you think I'll like," I say. "Thank you."

"My pleasure," he says. "Be right back."

He walks over to the neat, single-file line to order, and I direct my gaze out the window. It seems so long ago that I was sitting on a bench and saw my six-year-old self walking toward me. The day of my six years of youth in high school is unimaginable to me. It couldn't have gone too horribly, considering Rye's acting pretty normal, but I'm sure she had an eventful day. I'm sure she panicked, cried, and embarrassed herself. Embarrassed me.

I see a ladybug on the outside of the window. And with the sight of the ladybug comes the memory of the time in second grade when I was the star of our class play. What the play was about is lost to me, but I remember with clarity that I was the little ladybug. My costume was just about the most adorable thing I've ever seen, and I was the only one who got to wear blush for rosy cheeks. At the time, makeup of any sort was seen as something only "big kids" could use, which made the privilege even more meaningful. I remember my locket would always get stuck in the velcro of my costume, but I would refuse to take it off. I remember being genuinely happy, being free.

But things are different now.

Sometimes, I feel like I'll never be able to find my years. I'll always be stuck wondering what from my many years of youth I'm missing, and what still lingers in my mind, constructing who I am. Tears fill my eyes as I watch the ladybug move across the window. Looking at my locket, I long to make another wish. I have one wish, one hope, and one necessity: I wish to always have the little ladybug with me. But I already used my one daily wish. I decided to go back to kindergarten, to deceive my youth. Returning my gaze to the window, I shatter into pieces upon realizing the ladybug is gone.

"You okay, Jess ?"

Rye sits back at the table with our coffee and food.

"Yeah, I um… I think I still have a little sulfur in my eyes."

"*Jess*," he says. "What's wrong?"

He knows me too well. I meet his gaze, and I know I have to tell him. But I can't.

"Was I acting weird today?"

"You mean, weirder than usual?" he asks, and we both smile. "You seemed a little off at school, but everyone has those days."

"I have a question."

"I have my best attempt at an answer."

"How exactly did I get sulfur in my eyes? I'm, uh… I'm starting to forget. It happened so fast."

"I think you just touched it with your hands, then took your safety goggles off and touched your eye."

"*Wow*, I'm stupid!" I exclaim. "Then what happened?"

"Well, you had to go to the eyewash, then Chloe took you to clean up in the bathroom," he says slowly, as if I otherwise wouldn't understand. I can tell he's trying to hide it, but in his eyes, I can see how confused he is. I would be too. "You don't remember? You're acting like you weren't even there."

I wasn't. Well, *I* was. But I wasn't.

"Um… the burning in my eyes distracted me? I guess I just forgot."

I take a sip of my coffee in the hopes he'll believe my lies, and he just stares at me. I stare back, and after a few seconds of silence, he speaks.

"You'll be okay, Jess."

He takes a cake pop out of a bag and hands it to me.

"I thought you'd like the salted caramel kind."

I love combining opposite flavors. It shows how two seemingly contradictory tastes can make something great.

"You thought right," I say. "When you think about it, cake pops are so interesting…"

We spend the next half hour eating sweets, drinking coffee, and discussing the philosophy of cake pops. And for a while, I don't let my years intrude on my thoughts. I don't think about high school, kindergarten, or what tomorrow could bring. My youth is free.

Rye gets up to throw away our trash, and while he's gone, his phone rings on the table. Seeing it's his mom, I answer.

"Hello, Mrs. Arthur!"

"Jessica, is that you? Why do you have Rye's phone? Is he okay? Are you okay? Did Rye—"

"We're fine."

Rye walks back to our table.

"Would you like to speak to Rye?"

"Actually, darling, now that you're here, I'd like to ask you something. It's kind of serious."

"Bring it."

"Okay, well... do you think Rye looks silly when he wears those ragged shoes? You know, the off-white ones that look older than I am? He thinks they're nifty, but I'm not so sure. What do you think?"

"I think if he thinks they're nifty, then they're nifty."

"Alright, whatever you say, Jessica," says Mrs. Arthur. "Would you like to come over for dinner tonight?"

"I would love to."

"Great! Now, may I speak to Rye, please?"

"Sure," I say, handing him the phone.

They talk for a few minutes, then Rye ends the call.

"It's 5:15 now. So if my mom picks us up in an hour, we would be at my house for dinner by 6:30," he says. "In the meantime, do you wanna go to the dock?"

"I would love to."

The dock is on a lake about a block from here. California is renowned for its beautiful, crowded beaches along the Pacific Ocean, but Rye and I prefer the quiet calm of the isolated dock on a little lake. Its few miles may be insignificant compared to the nearby ocean, but the freshwater creatures which dwell in its depth are oblivious of the magnificent sea. Their home is the only compass they perceive.

We spent our first date on the little dock feeding fish crushed potato chips then kayaking for hours. We've been visiting it a lot lately, and now, it's officially considered our spot, even though neither of us have made it so.

Rye and I leave Starbucks. All is quiet until he looks at me with a glimmer in his eyes.

"Wanna hear a joke?"

"When wouldn't I?"

"Why did the chicken cross the road?"

"No idea."

"To get to the beautiful girl's house. Knock, knock."

"Who's there?"

"The chicken."

"You make me smile."

"I'm glad."

At the lakeside, I relish the beauty of the place. The dock was made a couple of years ago, yet still looks brand new. The wood is smooth and the jetty is steady as could be. Thriving green grass surrounds the boardwalk, always perfectly mown even though I know of no one who mows it. We sit on the edge and dangle our feet over the water.

"Look what I brought," says Rye. He takes out a bag of potato chips.

"Food for our fish friends!" I say. "Thank you."

We often feed the fish after school, and there's one in particular we never fail to see. It's bright blue with green dots on the tail, one of the smallest fish we've seen in the lake. The others seem to push it around, so we always try to give it extra food. We call it Paul.

Rye and I take turns smashing the bag of chips until they're in fish-friendly pieces. I lean over the dock and look into the water. The wavering lake moves peacefully with the wind, and fish are gathered in clusters.

"There's a lot here today," I say. Rye looks into the water.

"I think I see Paul."

I reach into the chip bag and drop a single crumb into the water, hoping our favorite little fish will reach it first. Immediately, all the others rush toward it, and one of the bigger ones swallows it.

"Sorry, little guy," I say. All the other fish stay in the general area where the first chip landed, but Paul swims off to the side, so when I drop another potato chip crumb, he's the first to reach it.

"That's one smart fish," says Rye. He grabs a handful of crumbs and tosses them in the water, and the fish devour them in seconds.

"Look," I say, pointing. Out of nowhere, a swan flies toward us and lands in the water. The fish scatter away, and the swan looks directly at the bag of chips.

"Here you go," I say, throwing a couple of crumbs in the water. The swan doesn't even move.

"Maybe it just wants to hang out with us," says Rye.

"I mean, we *are* pretty fun to hang out with, but I think these chips are the company it's after."

The swan swims in small circles, slowly approaching us. Once it gets close enough to the dock, it jumps onto the platform, taking us by surprise.

"Here you go, swan, you win," says Rye, dropping a handful of crumbs onto the dock. But instead of accepting them, the swan snatches the bag from Rye's hand and jumps back into the water.

I can't take my gaze off the intrepid creature.

"That's one savage swan!"

"A ninja, too," says Rye. "You know you have skill when you manage to snatch food from me."

"I know, I've tried. That swan is more athletic than I am."

six-year-old self was this morning, but he doesn't need to act upon this curiosity. He has a brother who can tell him all he wants to know about high school.

"When I was your age, I thought teenagers were the coolest people around," says Rye. "I thought all of them were role models for who I wanted to be. And then I got to high school."

Dustin looks at him with wide eyes. "You mean, some big kids aren't even a little cool?"

"Unfortunately not," says Rye. "But don't worry, Dustin; you'll be a cool big kid. I know you will. But for now, you should only worry about being a cool kindergartener."

"I think I'll be a lot cooler as a big kid than a kindergartner," says Dustin, a glimmer of hope in his eyes. "Everyone knows big kids are way cooler than kindergarteners."

"I know a lot of big kids who aren't nearly as cool as you, Dustin," I say. "Age doesn't get to decide how cool you are."

"Maybe it can't," says Dustin, yet he seems unconvinced. "Is high school gonna be a nightmare like everyone says?"

"Who says that?" asks Rye.

"A lot of the kids in my class say that," says Dustin with a frown. "They say high school has the most difficult work ever, and all the teachers are mean, and everyone fails."

"What do kindergarteners know about being in high school?"

"I never thought about it like that!" says Dustin, his bright smile returning. "They don't know anything at all."

Except for the six-year-old Jessica Jule Locke. But Dustin seems happy enough with his years.

"Do you think high school is awful?"

"Not at all."

"What about you, Jess?"

"I think you'll like high school. But remember: you're only in kindergarten. You have many years left before you have to worry about it."

"I'm glad I'm in kindergarten," says Dustin with ceremonious dignity. "I know big kids don't get recess!"

Unless you're a year-deceiving creature who can't seem to let go of her youth.

"You know, you kind of remind me of your older brother as a kindergartener," I say to Dustin. My years never seem to know when to stop.

"You remember what I was like in kindergarten?" asks Rye. "I don't even remember what I was like back then. You have a good memory."

Or maybe just a lost sense of youth.

"Is that a good thing?" asks Dustin.

"It's wonderful. Rye is definitely a big kid you should look up to."

Rye and Dustin both look at me and smile, reminding me of my life in my real years, and my day in kindergarten.

Mrs. Arthur drives me home, and as I wave goodbye, I feel at ease. Full of joy and rid of the burden of my years feeling false, I open my front door and greet my family. My mom and dad are watching TV with my twin ten-year-old brothers, Jacob and Jerry. My parents appear to be uninterested, but my brothers are engaged in a cartoon show, laughing at every punchline, as ten-year-olds do. As soon as I join them, they immediately turn toward me.

"Jess," says Jacob out of the blue. "Do all teenagers get to go out at night like you do?"

"And do all of them get to have a boyfriend or girlfriend?" asks Jerry.

"Do all of them have lots of friends?"

"Are all teenagers cool?"

They both sit up straight, leaning toward me. I smile. But as soon as I think about the questions, my thoughts edge toward sorrow.

"Think about it this way," I say. "Do all kids watch cartoons?"

"No," my brothers respond simultaneously.

"Are all kids twins?"

"Of course not!" says Jerry. "Jacob and I are special."

"Yes, you are, in more ways than one. It's the same with teenagers. Everyone is different, and age doesn't change that."

"That makes sense, I guess," says Jacob. "When I'm a teenager, I'm going to make sure I have lots of friends."

"And I'll go to all sorts of cool parties!" says Jerry. "When will we get to do those things, Jess? How old will we have to be?"

"The answer is different for everyone. It depends on your own view of your years," I say. "For now, just enjoy being young. And when you're old, you can enjoy being old."

Maybe I should take my own advice. My mind says yes, but my years say no. And my youth is indecisive.

"I have one more question," says Jacob. "When we're teenagers, can we still watch cartoons?"

"Of course you can," I say. "You can watch cartoons as long as you please."

No one speaks for a moment, but with the topic of youth, the conversation never ends.

"Jerry's full name has the word 'old' in it," says Jacob, laughing. "Jer*OLD*. Hey Jer*old*, how old—"

"That just means I have an older, wiser soul, *duh*. And my name is better than yours anyways" says Jerry. "I can't wait to be a teenager."

"You're going to have to," I say. "In the meantime, live your ten years of youth. And watch your cartoons."

After about an hour of switching between going on my phone and watching TV, I say goodnight to my family and head upstairs early. Today has been tiring, to say the least.

Once I'm ready for bed, I put my phone on silent, then turn off the light. As my head hits the pillow, I think about how lucky I am. I'm sure when I was younger, I never imagined my life to be like this. I'm sure I imagined myself as a princess in a castle, with every part of every day bright and filled with magic. But I never would have imagined my life to be this amazing.

I lie in darkness and look at the ceiling. The glowing stars I put up when I was younger remain there, and I stare at them every single night. Sometimes, I even make a wish. But I don't want to make another wish today. It's hard to make wishes when you're genuinely happy. Right now, my joy is genuine, yet in my false years, everything is fake. So I look at the glowing stars and think, am I happier now, or when I was younger? Will I be happier in ten years?

Earlier today, I wished to be younger, and my six years of youth wished to be older. And there's something wrong with that. I know there is.

It won't last forever, and truly, it shouldn't even have lasted for a minute. But it did. There's something wrong with wanting something you can't have. It's like a little ball of envy inside of you that can never truly be destroyed. Looking at the stars, I try to clear my head. Why worry about the negatives when you can be joyful over the positives? It would be like purposefully moving away from where you want to go. But then again, how are you supposed to change a bad situation if it doesn't upset you? Today, I've learned that my youth feels lost. I need to find it.

I look at the stars and think about all the things I'm not going to think about. Then I close my eyes and sleep, only to be woken by questions.

9

6 years of youth

The sound of babies crying wakes me, and my dream is

interrupted. I can't remember what it was about, but I picture a sky that doesn't look quite right. When I get out of bed, it takes me a moment to remember my age. I'm a kindergartener, and I own six years. Ever since I met my older self, everything has felt different. Wrong.

For whatever reason, Jacob and Jerry are always crying. They share a room next to mine, so when they sob, I get no sleep. It seems like they're never happy.

With the help of my parents, the twins eventually quiet down, and they fall back into whatever it is six-month-olds dream about. I'm far too old to remember, so my imagination can only guess. Being so much older, I know they look up to me. They probably wonder what it's like to be six. My little brothers don't even have to go to school for years yet! All they do is eat, sleep, and cry. It must be so nice. Yet it must be so boring.

Now that I'm awake, I see no point in returning to my dreams right away. It's way past my bedtime, and the rest of my family is asleep. Chloe tells me that big kids get to stay up as late as they want, even on school nights! And that's just not fair. In a way, I'm much older now. It doesn't matter that my false years can't reach me at home.

I step out of bed and carefully open my door. The house is dark and silent, and I struggle to sneak down the stairs. The rules my parents remind me of constantly don't matter anymore. Everyone knows that big kids don't follow rules. And right now, I don't feel so little.

No going downstairs after dark without a parent.

Walking slowly, I can't help but smile. I don't need a wish to act like a big kid. I'm a high schooler now! My locket is not nearly as powerful as I am. Thinking of how much I admire the sixteen-year-old me, I stretch the limits of my six years.

The corner of the couch that usually belongs to my brothers is where I choose to sit, simply because I can. Their box of toys takes up too much space, so I move it to the floor, knocking some out in doing so. I can't be bothered to pick them up. Instead, I dump out the box to see if there's anything I might want. A ladybug stuffed animal catches my eye, so I grab it and leave the rest of the toys in a mess on the floor.

No playing with your brothers' toys.

For the first time today, I have the TV all to myself. When I turn it on, the same dumb show my brothers always watch plays loudly, so I quickly turn down the volume. I change the channel to my favorite cartoon, but something about it seems different. I'm far too old for this. Eager to prove that my years can't stop me, I turn to a show my parents say I'm not allowed to watch until I'm a teenager. But they're not here right now. And I've earned far more privileges than I've been given.

No watching TV after eight.

No watching big kid shows.

The new show isn't nearly as interesting as cartoons, but I won't change the channel. If I can't prove to others that I'm not just a stupid little kid, I at least have to prove it to myself. And I know my older years are here somewhere. They always will be.

After a few minutes of boredom, I get up from the couch and tiptoe to the kitchen. I'm not hungry, and I've already brushed my teeth, but I can't let this opportunity go to waste. When I see a giant bag of M&Ms at the top of the fridge, I climb onto the counter and stand shakily, trying to keep my balance while reaching for the candy. I extend my arm far enough to grab the bag, then jump back to the floor. I get a glass bowl from a cabinet I'm barely tall enough to reach. Smiling, I pour in half the bag, not caring as I spill some on the floor. Only my parents use the glass dishes because they think I'll break them. But I'm not that stupid. And I'm not going to listen.

I move back to the couch, kicking aside all the toys on the ground. This new proud feeling is almost as sweet as the M&Ms.

No standing on the counter.

No using glass bowls.

No eating candy without asking first.

No—

"Jessica?"

My mom's voice is a whisper, but her tone sounds like a shout. I quickly turn off the TV and meet her eyes. It looks like she hasn't slept in days.

"I'm sorry!"

But I'm not. This was the plan. This is what I want.

"I... I get to stay up if I want to," I say slowly, crossing my arms. "I'm too old for a bedtime."

My mom turns on the lights, but I can still see the darkness outside.

"Look at the mess you've made!" she says, narrowing her eyes. "You know better. You'll clean this up tomorrow."

"But that's not fair! I—"

"*Shhh!* Be quiet or you'll wake up the twins."

I eat one more M&M when my mom isn't looking.

"You have to go to bed now, Jess. You don't want to be tired in school tomorrow."

School. High school. Hopefully.

"I'm excited for tomorrow," I say, barely whispering. I think only my years heard me.

I don't usually like staying up late, but the big kid me probably does. Maybe I should ask her. But I'm not sure if she wants to talk to me.

My mom and I walk upstairs as quietly as we can so we don't wake up the two little youths in the room next to mine. The sky is dark with clouds covering the stars, so I turn on my night-light to make sure no monsters can reach me. Chloe tells me night-lights are for babies, so I always lie and say I don't use mine anymore. Now I have no idea how to follow the rules of age. I break many and listen to few.

As I close my eyes and fall asleep again, I dream of colors trapped in an old, dull rainbow.

16 years of youth

My alarm wakes me from dreams of the brightest colors.

It's 6am, and even though I have to get up for school, my mind feels joyful and free of worries. When I turn on my phone, I see one missed message from Rye at 5:30am.

Rye: *Happy Valentine's Day!!! See you at school.*
Jess: *See ya!*

He often texts me early in the morning when he knows I'm not yet awake, because he knows it will be the first thing I see when I wake up. Never have I met anyone more thoughtful.

As I get ready, for a moment, I forget that yesterday I decided to spend the day in my six-year-old self's skin. My years will switch today, once again. So instead of a long, strenuous day at high school, I'll have another day of easy, carefree lessons in kindergarten.

A smile spreads across my face, but is wiped away as soon as it forms. Rye. I won't get to see him at school today. Sure, I'll see his six-year-old self, but to my sixteen, that's not really him. It's him at another time. A time when he doesn't know of our memories, our connection, our years. And Rye won't see me at school today either. To make matters worse, today isn't just any day; it's Valentine's Day. I know he has a surprise for me, a surprise my six-year-old self won't be able to fully appreciate.

I prepare for a day wasted, a day that could have been magical without a wish. But perhaps a good wish can undo a bad one. So I open my locket. I have one wish, one hope, and one necessity.

"I wish to go to high school today. Yesterday, when I wished to stay in my false years, it was a horrible mistake. My six-year-old self shouldn't have power over me. I wish to spend this Valentine's Day as me."

I close my locket.

***

When I get off the bus, I push past clusters of teenagers and bolt over to the grass between the high school and kindergarten. To no surprise, I see my six years of youth standing there, but I know with certainty that no one else can see us. Our years don't match.

My locket buzzes. I open it and read its message.

I heard your wish without a hitch / but it is not my choice whether or not you switch

I re-fold the piece of paper and avoid eye contact with my six-year-old self. I want to be able to spend the day in high school with the people I know. I want to be the one who gets to receive Rye's

Valentine's Day surprise, instead of the experience being granted to my faulty years. I want to talk to Chloe as her present self, not the six-year-old. I want to experience the previously obscured joys of high school, once again. I need be able to take back my wish.

I'm the only one with the power to make that change. But my younger years are a part of me, so they also have a say. My youth is stubborn. All the wishing in the world couldn't overrule my six-year-old self's power. My locket is incapable of granting such hopeless requests.

I face my six years of youth. She holds her locket steadily.

"We have to get this over with," I tell her. "School starts soon."

"What do you mean?"

"I mean we have to say goodbye now!" I say, tapping my foot. "I'll go back to high school, you'll go back to kindergarten, and this whole mess will be over."

"But I don't wanna go back to kindergarten," she says, playing with her frizzy, curly hair.

"Why not?"

"Well…" she says, staring at the ground. "The work is hard in high school, but it's a lot more interesting. And yesterday, we watched a movie in two different classes! Mrs. Rose never lets us do that! And we don't have to walk through the halls in a neat, single-file line like we do in kindergarten, and we get to—"

"But what about *me?*" I ask. "I can't stand another day of kindergarten!"

She gives me a nonchalant shrug.

"It was your wish."

"Just grow up and go back to kindergarten where you belong!" I snap, becoming more and more angry with myself.

"But to grow up, I have to go to high school more!"

"You're six! You'll be a wreck if you continue high school! And don't you miss recess?"

"Recess is overrated."

"What about stickers and Mrs. Rose?"

"Stickers are stupid and I like your teachers better than Mrs. Rose."

"I don't think it's a good idea for you to stay," I say, shaking my head. "Finals week is soon. That means lots of tests, studying, and hard work."

Finals in February? Lies.

"The locket will tell me the answers," she says, playing with the heart-shaped, silver locket around her neck.

"Not for a whole test, it won't. Trust me, I've tried."

"I can handle it."

"I can barely handle it, and I'm more than twice your age! Also, if you start failing high school, as any six-year-old would, Mom will stop packing yummy lunches and pack only vegetables instead."

Lies.

"Rye will share his food with me," says my six years of youth. "He's nice like that."

"Well... in high school, if you get one bad grade, you have to live in a box."

Lies.

"Then I won't get any bad grades!"

"Oh, trust me, you will!"

"Whatever. I'm gonna stay in high school whether you like it or not!"

"Six-year-old girls who go to high school don't get tooth fairy money!"

"I don't believe in the tooth fairy! Remember?"

Oh... how could I forget?

No matter how long it takes, I need to keep trying. I need to be me again.

"High schoolers don't get to watch TV before bed."

Lies.

"I'll deal with it!"

"Just *please!*" I implore. "Let's go to school where we belong."

"No," she says, crossing her arms.

"Yes!"

"No!"

"Please?"

"No!"

I sigh and shake my head at the irony of this whole situation. Here I am arguing with and lying to my youth. How can I ever trust anyone if I can't even trust myself? Sometimes, it takes a good look in the mirror to discover the goodness and the evil in others. Today, I've been mean to my six-year-old self. I've been mean to my many years of youth.

My six years of youth shakes her head and offers me her locket. As I realize I have no choice, tears of frustration form without warning. I take it and reluctantly hand her mine, and just like yesterday, the ground spins. Within seconds, I'm morphed into her body, and she is in mine. I wear her bright-colored princess t-shirt and purple pants, and she wears my top with a simple black and white pattern paired with blue jeans. My youth walks toward the high school, and I walk toward the kindergarten.

6 years of youth

I am such a meanie. Well, actually, *I'm* not. But she is. And she is me.

The big kid me won't take no for an answer. She won't listen. It's as if she never spent a day in kindergarten.

This was her wish just as much as it was mine. It seems like forever ago I walked up to the pretty girl sitting by herself on the high school bench. The first day of the switch, she seemed happy to be back in my place. I guess now she misses big kid Rye. How sad.

This is definitely not sad for me. I think I could get used to being with big kid Rye. To start, his face is a lot better in high school than it is in kindergarten. And in high school, he wears blue more, which I think looks better than the cartoon shirts he wears in kindergarten. Most of all, in high school, I matter to him. I'm his *girlfriend*! We're practically married!

It's Valentine's Day. I know he'll give me chocolate, flowers, and maybe even more! That would never happen in my real years. Rye will talk to me a lot today, because I am his girlfriend, after all. And this is high school. My years have done me well.

Today, I won't be stuck in boring old kindergarten; I'll be in an exciting, first-ever high school Valentine's Day adventure! And who would want to miss out on that?

Not my sixteen-year-old self, for sure. When will she ever learn?

It must be so boring being a big kid in kindergarten, so I can see why she didn't want to stay another day. And I'm sure she wanted chocolate and flowers from Rye too. At least she'll get them when we switch back at the end of the day, because I know they're not mine to keep. Maybe I'll even save a couple pieces of the chocolate for her instead of eating it all myself. I do feel bad for her, but she wished this on herself.

She might not be as smart as I thought.

When I walk into the high school, I see it's not as crowded as it was yesterday, and I wonder where all the big kids went and where the small groups I do see walking around are going. But instead of following them, I sit on the same bench I saw the big kid me sitting on yesterday. It's next to a big, half-open window, and the sun shines through and lights up the area around me. As soon as I sit down, my locket buzzes. I open it and unfold the piece of paper inside.

Day 4

Class 1: Spanish, room #301: 8:00-9:00

Class 2: Trigonometry, room #209: 9:05-10:05

Class 3: English, room #209: 10:10-11:10

Class 4: History, room #204: 11:15-12:15

Lunch: 12:20-12:55

Class 5: Art, room #112: 1:00-2:00

And now I'm confused. That didn't take long. This is high school, after all.

Why would the schedule change? The one yesterday worked perfectly fine. In this new schedule, one of the classes I had yesterday is gone, and two classes are new. Everything was so much simpler in kindergarten. But simple is boring.

Because I have nothing better to do, I just sit on the bench and watch as big kids pass by. It's actually interesting. All of them look different to me, and they seem to know where they're going. Most of them are talking to other big kids, and a few run along the halls as if there are no rules. After a minute of watching, I see a familiar face.

"Hi, Aimee!"

Aimee turns around and looks at me, and for some reason, she seems confused. She looks at a watch on her wrist.

"Hello, Jessica," she says slowly. "You do realize that the first bell doesn't ring for six minutes and thirty seconds, correct?"

"Oh, okay," I say. "Where did all the big kids go?"

"The *big kids*? I'm unaware as to—"

"I mean the non-little kids! High schoolers! Teenagers!"

For a few seconds, she just stares at me. I guess it's not normal to go to high school as a six-year-old. Nothing about this is normal.

"The reason why not many students are in this area of the building is that most people prefer to wait in the gymnasium, a fact that, in my exceptional opinion, should be utterly clear to you at this point in time. I've seen you and Chloe there on a multitude of occasions."

"Oh... yeah," I say, pretending to understand her. "So if I go down the stairs and into that big room, I'll find Chloe?"

"I would ask you if that sulfur has spread to your brain, but that would be illogical," says Aimee. "To answer your question: yes, you might find her."

"Cool!" I say. "Do you wanna come with me?"

"No, I most certainly would not," she says. Then, for the first time I've seen, she looks a little embarrassed. "What I meant to say was no, no thank you. People have been telling me I need to work on my manners."

Manners! I've been learning about those in kindergarten, with my real years!

"I can help you! I know a lot from Mrs. Rose."

"Mrs. Rose? You mean from kindergarten?"

Oh, no. I have to stop thinking like a six-year-old.

"No! I mean... yes! But I don't even remember much from *kindergarten.* You know, because it was *so* long ago. I'm not in kindergarten anymore. I'm in high school. Jessica Jule Locke is a *high schooler*, and I—"

"Yes, I am aware of your grade level."

Nailed it! My big kid disguise is even fooling Aimee.

"Good. Since we're both in high school, I can help you with manners. I like helping people."

"I suppose you're wise enough in the matter of being social that you are capable of answering my questions," says Aimee. "Starting with, why don't people seem to enjoy my jokes? Most would agree that telling jokes is a quality social skill; however, I feel as though nobody appreciates mine."

"Well, how about you tell me one?"

"Really?"

"Sure! I love jokes."

Aimee sits next to me on the bench and *smiles*! Being a big kid is getting more interesting the longer I am one.

"Alright, I believe I have a good one. Knock, knock."

"Who's there?"

"To."

"To who?"

"Actually, that's grammatically incorrect! I believe you meant to say 'to *whom*!'"

Aimee laughs more than I ever imagined possible.

"I don't get it."

"A common grammatical error is the use of 'who,' when instead the pronoun 'whom' is correct in order to refer to the object of a verb or preposition, and oftentimes—"

"I see your problem!" I say. "If you tell jokes that are too hard for people to understand, they won't be funny. You should only tell jokes you know everyone will get. Here's an example: knock, knock."

"Who's there?"

"Banana."

"Banana who?"

"Knock, knock."

"Who's there?"

"Banana."

Aimee rolls her eyes.

"This is redundant and lacks any perceptible purpose! I don't believe—"

"Just be patient. It's part of having good manners. Knock, knock."

"Who's there?"

"Banana."

"Banana who?"

"Knock, knock."

"Who's there?"

"Orange."

"Orange who?"

"*Orange* you glad I didn't say banana?"

"The word *orange* does not sound remotely similar to the contraction 'aren't,' a fact that should be obvious, as orange fails to rhyme with any word in the English language. Also, to my infallible knowledge, that joke was only perceived as funny in kindergarten."

Oh, no. The smartest person I know might be starting to see through my big kid mask. But at least I'm sort of helping Aimee. She's the smart one. And I'm only six.

I must be smarter than I thought.

"It's good manners to laugh at someone's joke, even if you didn't think it was funny."

"But for what reason—"

"Because it makes the other person happy. And if they're happy, you can be happier too. It doesn't matter that they tell lame jokes."

"I suppose that makes logical sense. May we try again?"

"Sure. Knock, knock."

"Perhaps, you should only say the concluding line."

"*Orange* you glad I didn't say banana?"

"Ha! Ha, ha! Ha!"

I think she's trying to fake a laugh, but it sounds like more of a snort mixed with a robot crying.

"What do you think?"

"You have to make it sound real. And don't actually say 'ha,' because that will sound too fake. And maybe—"

A bell rings overhead, and I look around to see mobs of big kids starting to fill the hallways. I know it's time for class, but I still want to help Aimee. I'm sure the real high school me would too.

"Do you want to come over to my house today? I can help you more, if you want."

"That appears to be the only logical decision," she says. "I'll bring food, as I am aware that such an action is a clear display of good manners, correct?"

"I guess so."

"Noted. I'll attempt to bring a food item that contains both nutritious and delicious qualities."

"Cool. I live at—"

"I already know your address. Would three o'clock be a convenient time?"

"Sure! See you then!"

She smiles what looks to me like a true smile, and we walk in different directions to our classes. As I leave the bench, I realize I won't be helping Aimee with her social skills after school today. I won't be there. My sixteen-year-old self will have to do that.

In the middle of the crowded hallway, I take my new schedule from my pocket and look at class number one. Apparently, I have Spanish, which is in room 301. Because I sometimes watch Dora, I know Spanish is a different language, and I'm even smart enough to know words like *hola*, *adios*, *sí*, and *uno*, *dos*, *tres*.

I go upstairs and find room 301 so quickly you'd think I'd been in this school for years. Walking into the classroom, I see that it looks the same as almost all of the big kid classrooms I've seen so far, other than all the posters with words I can't understand. I see Chloe sitting at a cluster of desks in the middle of the room, and she waves at me. Thankful for my best friend and all of her years, I sit next to her.

"Hey, Jess!" says Chloe. "Did you—"

She starts to ask me something, but stops when she sees a woman— the teacher, I think— look our way.

"Hola, amiga!"

"Hi Chloe," I say, wondering why she's already speaking in Spanish. Class hasn't even started yet! "I'm so happy it's Valentine's Day. Do you—"

"En Español, por favor!" yells the woman.

"What?"

"In Spanish, Jess," whispers Chloe.

Oh, no. Big kids are supposed to be able to actually *talk* in Spanish? Wow. My sixteen-year-old self does it all.

"Um... hola, Chloe!" I say, the panic already starting.

"Es el día de San Valentín! Comó estás?"

"Sí," I say, because it's one of the only things I know how to. I look over to see the teacher staring at us, so I try to repeat the last part of what Chloe said. "Clomo esus."

Chloe raises an eyebrow, probably because the real high school me isn't as stupid as I am. Before she has time to respond, the teacher walks to the front of the room.

"Hola, clase! Por favor, abre tus libros a la página ochenta y tres."

All of the big kids open the book placed on every desk, so I do the same. I flip to page 248, and the teacher looks at me and shakes her head.

"*Jess!*" whispers Chloe. "Page 83."

Trusting she knows what she's talking about, I go to page 83. The teacher smiles, but all I can do is frown. I hate this already. I hate this class, I hate being the stupid one. I hate that I decided to spend another day here.

The teacher starts reading in what sounds like gibberish, but the rest of the class seems to understand.

"Now we are going to watch a video on how to use present and past tense in Spanish."

English! I have never been so grateful for it. The teacher plays a video about something I, of course, don't understand. Maybe this is just what it's like to be in my wrong years. Maybe, high school as a kindergartener will always be like Spanish class.

After what seems like hours of whatever it is the video is about, a bell rings overhead. Looking at my schedule, I frown when I see "trigonometry" next.

How could I be so stupid?

16 years of youth

I trudge toward the kindergarten, wishing more than anything for the privilege of being me again, in my true years. I'm sure my six years of youth enjoys being with Rye, and she's sure to receive my Valentine's Day gift in high school. I'm sure she's pleased with herself.

As soon as I make it into the building, I see Mrs. Rose and Laura heading toward the all-too-familiar kindergarten classroom. I run to catch up, and take them by surprise.

"Jessica, sweetie, did you come in here all by yourself?" asks Mrs. Rose.

"Yeah," I say, rolling my eyes. "I don't need anyone to walk me in or hold my hand."

We enter the classroom, and I see almost all of the kindergarteners sitting in a circle on the rug. And now the teenager joins.

"Jess!" says Chloe. "Come sit here!" she points to an empty spot between her and Laura.

I walk toward her, but before I can sit, Laura moves her legs to cover the spot.

"No!" she says. "This is Mindi's spot. Why don't you sit next to *Rye*? And after that, you two can get *married*!"

I move to the empty space between Rye and Chloe instead. Rye turns toward me and smiles.

"Did you know that artichokes are actually flower buds that haven't bloomed?" he asks, a persistent glimmer of youth in his eyes. "But just because they're not like normal flowers, doesn't mean they're not awesome."

I almost cry.

Seeing him this young makes me miss the real him — the one in high school, who, because of my wish, I won't get to see for more than six hours. I think back to yesterday when he brought an artichoke to my door, then of our time at Starbucks, and the giving swan. And now it's Valentine's Day. I know he's going to give me a surprise at school, and I'm going to miss it. I'll most likely be doing something stupid, like playing a game or repeatedly learning what two plus two equals. I don't even want to think about how my six years of youth will react. It's all up to her and her childish ways. And the worst part is, I can't tell him. I can't explain to Rye that the person he sees at school today isn't the person he thinks it is. I can't tell him it's not me he sees, but my six years of youth with a mask. While we are genetically the same, our years define us.

Everything my kindergarten years do at high school today will be looked on as me. When Rye gives me whatever his surprise may be, I won't be able to even thank him. My six-year-old self will be the one to respond. She might complain that she wanted a pony, not flowers. She might hate it and cry. She could do anything, and I have no way of stopping her.

My youth is out of my control.

"Jess?" says Rye. "Are you okay?"

"No."

"Well, why not?"

"Because of so many different reasons that would take an eternity to explain, and by then, I'd have a whole new list."

"Um… I'm sorry," he says so awkwardly it's cute. "Do you wanna hear a joke?"

"I would love to."

"What do you call a sleeping dinosaur?"

"I have no clue."

"A dino*snore*."

"That's clever," I say. "I have one. What do you call a person who thinks Rye is awesome and caring and funny?"

"I don't know."

"Jessica Locke."

"That's your name!"

"It is."

"So, you mean, you think I'm awesome and caring and funny?"

"That's exactly what I think."

Rye smiles with all his six years, and Mrs. Rose addresses us kindergarteners.

"We have a fun day planned! Today is Valentine's Day, so to start, we'll be learning a bit about this special holiday!"

The class cheers, but I doubt this is going to be any better than yesterday. At least for me, it won't. Thinking about Valentine's Day fills me with dread.

"Who here knows what Valentine's Day is?"

Of course, Rye raises his hand.

"It's the day you show the person you love how much you love them."

"Good job! Does anybody know an example of a common Valentine's Day gift?"

Laura raises her hand.

"A pony?"

"No, not quite," says Mrs. Rose. "Think more common."

I raise my hand, because why not? I might as well be the smart one again if I'm going to be stuck here.

"Flowers and chocolate."

"There you go," says Mrs. Rose. "Now, everyone knows what date it is today, right?"

"Yeah, it's Valentine's Day. You already told us!" says a boy on the opposite side of the circle.

"No, honey, I mean, what calendar date is it today?"

The class goes silent, and my years feel on fire.

"February 14th!" I yell, losing my patience.

"That's correct, Jessica, but how about we raise our hands next time?"

"How about you ask a better question next time?"

"I don't like that tone, Jessica."

I press my lips together.

"And I don't like this class, Mrs. Rose."

"You're being very rude today. Don't expect any stickers any time soon."

"*Ooo-oooh!*" goes the class of kindergarteners.

Okay, Jess, calm down.

This is kindergarten. *Just* kindergarten. A place where a little attitude is a seen as a serious issue because the school system makes an effort to prevent us from growing up to be *bratty big kids*. I guess it's wise to start at a young age. But I'm already sixteen. This place can't change me. I won't let it. My years are beyond any kindergartener in this room, so it's only right I show my maturity.

I have my years and I'm not afraid to use them.

"I'm *scared*," I say, crossing my arms and looking Mrs. Rose directly in the eyes. Her expression of distressed astonishment makes it all worth it.

"I've had enough of that attitude, Jessica! You can sit in the time-out chair for the next five minutes," she says, pointing to a yellow chair in one corner of the classroom.

Standing up to move to the time-out chair, I see most of the kids in the class staring at me with wide eyes, and Rye and Chloe seem especially shocked. As I walk over to the chair, I hear Mrs. Rose mutter under her breath, "Where did that kid learn sarcasm?"

From my many years of youth, Mrs. Rose. That's where.

In the corner of the classroom, facing away from all the kindergarteners, I think about where I could be. I could be with Rye in high school this Valentine's Day, flowers in hand. I could be happy. I could be me.

And then the realization hits me: I'm a sixteen-year-old girl in kindergarten sitting in a time-out chair thinking about her mistakes. My tears arrive before I can even try to stop them.

10

<u>6 years of youth</u>

I f I was in my real years, it would be about time for recess.

Today's one of the few days Chloe will be at the playground, but her best friend won't be there. If I was where I should be, I would be playing outside, without a care, with my best friend. My real best friend, the one who's six. Instead, I'm here in high school trying to find a class I don't even know how to pronounce. I won't have recess today. I won't have playtime. The only thing left to like about today is that it's Valentine's Day. And my sixteen-year-old self has a *boyfriend*. I'm sure I'll get flowers, chocolate, and maybe even more! My false years could end up being a good thing, after all.

About half the seats in room #322 are full, and most of the big kids are talking with each other about whatever it is big kids talk about. I sit at a desk two rows from the front, but I have no one to talk to. So I just stare at the wall.

At least I haven't cried yet.

"Hey, Jess!"

I look away from the wall to see Chloe sitting next to me, and because she's here, I'm not so sad anymore.

"I'm *so* annoyed with Spanish class, aren't you? I mean, it's bad enough that we have to be taught using basically no English, but to make *us* only speak in the language we clearly don't know, because that's why we're learning it? It's crazy!"

"Sí," I say, trying to get her to think I actually know Spanish. Maybe if I'm smart enough to hide my real years, nobody will be able to tell how stupid I am.

"You're *so* funny, Jess," she says using a strange tone. "Have you seen Rye yet today?"

"Not yet. Do you think he'll give me chocolate? And flowers? I think chocolate is better, so I hope he got me a lot."

"He'll probably get you something more meaningful than that. What did you get him?"

"I didn't know I was supposed to get him anything."

Doesn't she know only the sixteen-year-old me was supposed to do that?

"*Jessica Jule Locke!*"

"Yeah?"

"It's Valentine's Day! And you guys have been dating for what, a year and a half?"

"Yes?"

"Then of course you need to get him something! He's your boyfriend! What, did that sulfur spread to your brain?"

That's now the second time today someone has asked me that.

"Come on, follow me!"

Chloe grabs my hand, and we both stand up.

"But we have class!"

"Just trust me!"

She walks toward the teacher who sits at his desk reading, and I follow her.

"Can I go to the nurse? My throat hurts," she asks, suddenly sounding sick. The teacher points at me.

"Why does she have to come with you?"

They both look at me, and for a second, I'm worried they can see my real years.

"I have a horrible sense of direction, and I always forget where the nurse is," says Chloe, her voice still strange.

"Just be back as soon as possible."

I follow Chloe as she slowly walks out of the classroom, then runs toward the stairs. Even though it's against the rules in kindergarten, I run with her. She is my best friend, no matter how my years may change. And this is high school.

We slow to a fast walk, and when I look at Chloe, I'm worried she'll get more sick.

"Just so you know, I have no idea where the nurse is."

"We're not going to the nurse, Jess," she says, her voice back to normal.

"But I thought—"

"I pretended to be sick so we could find you something to give to Rye. We won't get anything meaningful, of course, but we'll figure that out later," she says. "That's just how awesome I am."

"Won't we get in trouble?"

"Love comes before math. Come on, move faster!"

Once we make it to the second floor, Chloe turns her head like she's looking for something. We see a girl I recognize as Chelsea, the one whose seat I wasn't allowed to sit in yesterday, and Chloe runs toward her. I'm still confused, but I follow. Chloe is much smarter than me and my six years.

"Chelsea!"

Chelsea turns toward Chloe, but she doesn't look happy to see us.

"What do you want?"

"Jess here is in a little bit of a predicament, you see, she forgot to get a gift for Rye, so we were wondering if maybe—"

"*Wow*, Jessica!" says Chelsea, laughing as if something were funny. "I would hate to be you right now."

She walks away, still laughing.

"Rude!" yells Chloe. "Come on, Jess, we'll find someone else."

"What exactly do we need to find someone for?"

"It's Valentine's Day, so most people in relationships were probably smart and got gifts. So until you get something meaningful for Rye, a cliché, generic, no-good substitute will have to do. That is, if we can find one."

"But why—"

"Laura!"

We follow Laura into the girls' bathroom, but right now, I don't want to talk to her. She's never nice in kindergarten, and with ten more years, she's still awful. But right now, I'll do anything to help my big kid self.

Laura turns around and looks at us, then rolls her eyes. Chloe smiles, but her eyes look sad.

"Hi, Laura. Jess is in a bit of a situation. You see, she forgot to get a gift for Rye, so we were wondering if maybe you could help us by —"

"I always have an abundance of gifts for both my guy and girl friends," she says. "Because I have *a lot* of people who think I'm their best friend."

"*Congratulations*. Do you think you could be a savior and let Jess have one?"

"I could," says Laura. "But I won't."

"Why not?"

"I don't want to," says Laura, playing with her hair and looking at her perfectly painted nails. "Now leave."

gift on Valentine's Day. That's one reason we learn about it," I say, thinking about the gift I got Rye. I bought it a couple of months ago and saved it for today. Ideally, I'd be able to give it to him at school. High school. But nothing is ideal anymore.

"Or I could just eat chocolate all day," says Chloe. And now the big kid is the bearer of bad news.

"That's what a lot of people do, but I wouldn't suggest it."

"What about ice cream?"

"It's the same."

"Valentine's Day sounds pretty boring to me," says Chloe. "I think Christmas is better."

"I like Christmas better, too," I say, because I know I would have when I was truly her age. "Hey, Chloe, can I ask you something?"

"Does it have to do with Valentine's Day?"

"No."

"Then sure."

"Do you ever think about being a high schooler? You know, like the people in that building," I say, pointing to where I should be.

"All the time," she says. "I think about how awesome it will be, and how different, and how interesting. But I know it's gonna be a lot more work than kindergarten. Maybe high school is only for the smart big kids."

I try to think of a response to such a statement, but high school is a difficult subject to explain to a six-year-old.

"Jess," says Chloe, nudging my shoulder. "Look."

I see Rye walking toward us with a single blue tulip in his hand. When he notices we're looking at him, he waves and smiles.

"Hi, Jess!"

"*Ehh-emm!*" says Chloe, glaring at him.

"And Chloe," he says. "So, Jess, since it's Valentine's Day, I got you this flower from over there."

He points to a small area of nature next to the playground, then hands me the tulip.

"I hope you like it. And also, do you wanna sit with me at lunch again today?"

"Actually, she's sitting with *me* at lunch today. Better luck next time!" says Chloe with a sassy smile.

"I'll sit with both of you," I say, and Chloe's mouth falls wide open. "Thank you for the flower, Rye. That was very thoughtful of you."

"No problem," he says, avoiding Chloe's questioning eyes. "Well, I'll leave now. See you after recess!"

He walks back to the center of the playground, and I hold my blue tulip with a tenacious grip.

"Why didn't I get a flower?" asks Chloe, looking at the ground.

"I think Rye gave me this because I gave him a chocolate bar at lunch yesterday," I say, even though I know it's not true. "Don't worry, Chloe, I'm sure you would get lots of flowers if people had the courage to give them to you. Rye is very courageous, so that's why he gave me one."

"I'm nice to Rye. Well... at least I am sometimes. So how come he didn't give one to me too?"

"You can only give one person a flower on Valentine's Day. That's how it works," I say. Sometimes, I forget just how young six-year-olds are.

"Do you think one day, when I'm a big kid, someone will give me a flower?"

"I'm certain of it."

"But what about my scar?"

She points to the permanent mark on her nose that her cat gave her when she was three.

"It's beautiful, Chloe."

"It's ugly."

"It's beautiful."

"It's ugly! A scar can't be beautiful, only—"

"Chloe! Please, trust me. It's beautiful."

"Thanks, Jess," she says. "Your birthmark is beautiful too. It kinda looks like a giraffe! In a good way."

I chuckle, and our smiles mirror each other.

"So are you and Rye boyfriend and girlfriend? Tell me the truth."

"No," I say, because here in kindergarten, it's true. "Maybe someday when we're older."

"I think you guys would be great together as big kids," she says. "Will I be invited to your wedding?"

"Woah, Chloe," I say, laughing. "Let's not get too ahead of ourselves. But yes, if Rye and I ever do get married, you will most certainly be invited to our wedding."

"A *wedding*?"

I look away from Chloe to see Rye standing a few feet from the tire swing.

"I came back here because the boys over there were making fun of me for giving a girl a flower," he says, blushing. "Then I heard my name and something about a wedding. What were you saying?"

"Um... well, Chloe here was thinking far, *far* into the future, and she asked if she would be invited to our wedding. You know, *if* we ever got married," I say. "But don't worry, I'm fully aware we are only in kindergarten."

Rye looks at me with an expression of everlasting curiosity. Looking at him now, it's hard to believe I know him as sixteen. His kindergarten youth gives the impression of a boy who could never grow old, an immortal youth and soul that could never weaken. But growing up is a choice given to no one.

Rye looks into my eyes.

"So, when's the wedding?"

"Um… let's see," I say, thinking carefully.

He looks at me as if waiting for an answer that would change his life. So I give him one with the full realization it can't be real. But I no longer have much of a distinction between false and true, impossible and unimaginably great.

"If we ever get married, I would like for it to be in December. What day in December would you want it to be?"

"December 12th," he says without hesitation. "I'll remember that. See you after recess, Jess!"

He skips back to the center of the playground.

"I don't know if I approve," says Chloe. "Do you really want your wedding that close to Christmas?"

"Exactly."

"How many years do you think it will be until you guys get married? I mean, *if* you guys get married."

"Many. But remember, Chloe, we have many years of youth left before we have to worry about that stuff. We still have the rest of kindergarten, high school, college, and everything in between. We have time."

"I'll remember that," says Chloe. "By the way, I think your wedding dress should have sparkles on it. That way, it will shine in the sun."

"I'll remember that," I say. And I will.

11

6 years of youth

I'll always remember my first day of kindergarten.

About half a year ago, I remember thinking that being able to finally go to kindergarten was the most exciting thing in the world. I had heard all sorts of stories about what kindergarten would be like, so the night before I walked into the building I belong in now, I could barely sleep.

That first day, my years felt at home. Nothing felt out of place like it does here in high school. Then, my years had no reason to lie.

My kindergarten self was happy being my kindergarten self. I know the person I was then would be impressed to know I went to high school yesterday. But the person I am today doesn't know how to feel anymore. I now know that I will have two first days of high school. Yesterday was one of them, a day I will never forget. And someday, when I'm actually a teenager, I'll have my second first day of high school. My real first day. And I'll be me. My mind, my body, my years— all mine.

Today is my second English class with the big kids, and only a few people are in the classroom when I reach it. One of them is the rude girl from yesterday, and for a moment, I almost sit next to her. I want to prove that I'm not scared, that I can sit wherever I want, even though I am secretly only six. But instead, I sit in the same spot as yesterday. A kindergartener has no business taking a high schooler's seat. I don't belong here, anyways.

"Hey, Jess!"

Kayla and Kora walk into the classroom and take the two seats in front of me.

"Have you seen Rye yet?" asks Kora.

"Tell us everything!" says Kayla.

They look at each other and smile, then stare at me. It seems to me that the two of them have more in common than I do with my own sixteen-year-old self. They look the same, talk the same, and they are both nice, social, and completely perfect. Then there's me and my years. We're nothing alike.

"I haven't seen him yet," I say, and they both frown. "I don't think I'll see him until lunch."

"That's perfect!" says Kayla, her smile coming back. "There is nothing more romantic than food!"

"Do you think he's gonna do something big?" asks Kora.

"Maybe read you a poem in front of everyone?" asks Kayla.

"Or give you something super thoughtful?"

"I can't wait!"

"Me neither!"

I have no idea why they care so much about this. They're way more excited than I am, and I'm the one who's getting whatever it is I'm going to get. Maybe I'm just not old enough to understand.

"I'm excited too," I say.

"What did you get him?" asks Kayla.

Oh, no. Hopefully, they won't have the same reaction Chloe did. But now, I have a lie, a lie to help me lie about my years.

"Um… I think I'm saving up to get him a good birthday gift. Yes, that's it!"

"I'm okay with whatever," I say, because I know I won't be there. It's my sixteen-year-old self I have to think about. "But maybe not anything that has to do with Valentine's Day. I don't think I'd like that."

"Noted."

"What are you getting food for?" asks Chloe.

"Jessica is going to help me improve on my social skills."

"You know, I've been told by a certain person by the name of Jessica Locke that I excel at the fine art of social skills."

"You can help us, Chloe," I say. I'm sure the sixteen-year-old me would be happy to see her real best friend again after a boring day of kindergarten. "Kayla, Kora, do you guys wanna come too?"

They both agree.

"Cool! You can come over at three."

"When is Rye stopping by?" asks Chloe.

I almost forgot about that. If only I had the mind of a big kid, this would be a lot simpler.

"Um… I don't know. When he does, you guys can just hide in my room… or something like that. And if you want—"

"The turkey has roasted! I repeat, the turkey has roasted!" says Chloe.

"What do you—"

"Rye is coming!"

I see Rye walking toward our table, and my heart beats faster than it has as long as I've been in high school. He looks at me and smiles, and once I remember Chloe's advice, I give him a shy smile back. Rye reaches the table, and I take a deep breath.

"Happy Valentine's Day, Jess!" he says, reaching out to give me a hug. I stand up next to him.

"Thanks," I say. Then I remember the words of my locket. "You get your gift after school. Oh, and take this card."

He reads the card and laughs a little, but I don't know why he thinks it's funny. Then he reaches into a colorful bag.

"It's great, Jess. Here, I got you these."

He gives me a bundle of blue tulips, and I'm not quite sure what to do with them. I try to put them in my backpack, but it takes a few moments because they barely fit.

"Do you want anything in return?" I ask, remembering my manners. "I don't have your gift now, but I guess I could try to find something."

"You don't have to do that. You've already given enough."

"But Mrs. Rose says it's polite to give back when you receive."

Rye raises an eyebrow, and I realize my mistake right away.

"Mrs. Rose? You mean from kindergarten?"

"No, *of course not!*" I say. Before he can ask me any more questions, I quickly change the subject. "Anyways... you're sure I've already given enough?"

"Most certainly," he says. Looking into his eyes, I see the faint glow of his kindergarten years, but when I blink, it goes away. "I have something special for you."

He takes a small, silver box from his bag and hands it to me. It looks too small to be chocolates, but maybe he'll give those to me later. I open the box to see a silver charm bracelet. When I put it on my wrist, I notice it has a charm that says "Jess," one that says "Rye," a weird shape I think is an artichoke, a star, a mini version of the locket around my neck, and a swan. I try to hide my disappointment. I have no idea why big kids like jewelry so much, but I think it's boring.

"Thanks," I say, playing with my hair and avoiding his eyes. When I look up at him, Rye looks disappointed, but I don't know why.

"I picked it up last night after you came over for dinner. Most of the charms I've had custom-ordered for months now, and a few I bought yesterday as extras, like the swan and the artichoke. The jeweler was about thirty miles from here. It's all real silver with professionally crafted charms, and—"

"That's cool," I say, getting bored with listening to him. Maybe he has something more interesting, like the chocolate Chloe was saying he might have. "Did you get me chocolate?"

"Really?" he asks, frowning.

"Really what?"

"All you have to say is 'thanks' and ask for chocolate?"

"Yeah! I... I think that's all," I say, but I'm not sure what he means. "What about cookies? I know you usually have those."

He just stares at me, and even though the room is packed with noisy big kids, all I can hear is his silence.

"As long as they're not oatmeal raisin, any kind of cookies are good," I say, trying to lighten the mood.

"I put a lot of thought into that," he says, looking at the ground.

"So you *do* have cookies!"

"Do you even— *nevermind*, Jessica! I have to go."

Without meeting my eyes, he turns and starts to walk away.

"Why are you leaving?"

He faces me again, then looks at me with an expression I have never before seen on him. Maybe it's just my years.

"I just thought you would appreciate the bracelet more. But you don't even care," he says. "This isn't like you at all."

"But you didn't follow the script!"

"What are you *talking* about?"

"The script! Chloe and I had a script! And you didn't follow it like you were supposed to! So who's fault is it now?"

"That doesn't make any sense!" he says. "Are you trying to blame *me*?"

"Yes!"

163

I have to blame someone. And right now, I don't want it to be my years.

"Are you serious? What is wrong with you today?"

"I'm sorry!" I say. As I remember the Valentine's Day history I learned about in class, my heart beats faster. "Please don't chop my head off!"

Lots of big kids at tables around us turn to look at me, and they look as shocked as I was when I realized the high school me has a boyfriend. Many of them whisper to each other, point at us, and even laugh, which, by now, I'm used to. I know the feeling of making a fool out of myself all too well. The room becomes quieter, and Rye's face turns red.

"I have to go, Jessica," he says, turning away from me before I can respond.

I watch as he leaves the room, and as he does, the noise in the cafeteria returns. When I turn toward the girls at the table, they all stare at me with wide eyes. Chloe doesn't look happy at all.

"What was *that*?" she asks.

"What do you mean?"

"*Thanks*? That's all you had to say? And asking for chocolate and cookies? Jess, that was awful!"

"I didn't know I'm not supposed to ask for food! And Mrs. Rose says it's polite to say 'thanks!'"

"Mrs. Rose? What are you talking about?"

"I don't even know!" I say, because here in high school, all I am is stupid. "*I just want to go home!*"

Everyone at the table looks at me like I'm crazy. But it was only my wish.

"What has been up with you, Jess?" asks Chloe. "Monday you were fine, but today and yesterday you've been acting like a completely different person."

"Maybe that's just what high school does to me!"

"We've been high schoolers for more than a year and a half now! I'm pretty sure if you were gonna have a high school based crisis, it would have happened already!" says Chloe. "Poor Rye. He must be devastated."

"I didn't mean to!" My eyes fill with tears of guilt and confusion.

"Of course you didn't," says Chloe, speaking more calmly. "I know you would never do anything to hurt Rye on purpose, but you still have to apologize."

"But I don't even know what I'm sorry for," I say, blinking the tears away.

"When someone buys you something, especially something thoughtful or expensive, you don't just say thanks! You tell them how much you love and appreciate it. That is definitely not the right time to ask for food! And *never* mention our practice scripts! Remember when I got you that purse for your birthday last year, and you kept thanking me for hours? You're never ungrateful."

Maybe the sixteen-year-old me is never ungrateful. But I'm not her.

"Don't worry, Jess," says Kayla. "I'm sure he'll understand if you talk to him."

"Tell him why the past few days have been weird," says Kora. "I know he'll listen to you."

"Then everything will be okay," says Kayla. "And your day will be just a little less than perfect."

"Yes, the outcome of this situation should not be too terribly unfortunate," says Aimee, nodding her head slowly. "It is scientifically proven that over 97% of high school relationships don't last anyways."

"*Aimee!*" says Chloe. "Don't be sad, Jess. Rye will forgive you, because I know you can fix this. You're a smart girl."

"I have my next class with Rye," says Kayla. "I'll tell him how sorry you are and how guilty you feel. Sound good, Jess?"

"Sure," I say. "Thank you all for being so nice."

"We're here for you," says Chloe. "I'll bring mini donuts to your house after school today, because I know they make you smile."

"I'll bring ice cream," says Kayla.

"I'll bring chocolate sauce, sprinkles, and whipped cream," says Kora.

"Well, I do like food," I say, the frown leaving my face. I'm sure my sixteen-year-old self would appreciate having them bring treats. After what just happened, I definitely owe her.

"Can we play games while you guys are over? I think I'd like that."

"Of course, whatever you wish," says Chloe. "But no homework! Just food and friends."

Maybe it will be fun. But I won't be there. I won't know. My sixteen-year-old self will be there with her high school friends.

No kindergarteners allowed.

A bell rings overhead, and everyone starts to leave the lunchroom.

"See you later, Jess," says Kayla.

She and Kora wave, and even Aimee gives me a smile. Chloe and I walk through the crowded hallways with her slightly ahead of me, because we both have art next, but I have no idea where it is. I don't know anything.

"Don't worry, Jess. Rye will understand."

"I hope he does," I say. If not for me, for my sixteen years of youth.

12

<u>16 years of youth</u>

For the sake of my six years of youth, I hope this isn't the best

kindergarten has to offer.

Thinking back to my real kindergarten days, I remember them being much more intriguing and lively than this trick. I remember waking up and feeling genuinely excited for a day at school— certainly a lot more excited than I am to go to high school these days. And sometimes, when the day was over, I wouldn't want to leave kindergarten. Considering I'm here ten years later, I guess I never truly left my early years of youth behind. In my real days of kindergarten, everything was different. Everything seemed perfectly in place. Maybe it's just me.

Us kindergarteners grab our lunch boxes and form a neat, single-file line at the door. Rye and Chloe stand beside me. They look into my eyes, then at each other, and I can sense the tension between them. But to my surprise, neither say a word.

We walk through the quiet, lonely halls until we reach the same small lunchroom as yesterday. I sit at a circular table, and Chloe and Rye sit on either side of me. For a few moments, all three of us remain silent. Then Chloe turns toward Rye.

"So, Rye," she says, crossing her arms, "Why do you think you're better than Superman?"

Rye tilts his head.

"What do you mean?"

"I *mean*, in what ways do you believe you are better than Superman? It's a simple question!" she says. "Jess deserves to marry the best boy in the world, and I'm not sure if you make the cut. I think Superman is way better than you, but being the kind person I am, I will allow you two minutes— not one second more— to convince me otherwise. Go."

Rye freezes.

"Um... I c-can—"

"Don't stutter!"

"Okay, well... I'm nice."

"You can't fly like Superman."

"I tell funny jokes. Like that dinosaur one I told Jess, remember —"

"You can't save the world like Superman."

"I'm smart... I think."

"Superman has a better sense of fashion than you."

"I—"

"Your two minutes is over!"

"But it's only been—"

"*Shhh!*"

For a moment, the three of us are silent. Chloe looks at Rye, then at me.

"I don't think this is working out," she says, shaking her head. "I'm sorry, Rye. Better luck next time! You're welcome, Jess."

Rye stands.

"Jess and I are friends, and there is nothing you can do about it! You are no longer invited to our wedding!"

Chloe jumps to her feet, jabbing a finger at Rye.

"But you don't have muscles like Superman! And you don't have an awesome red cape! But your face will sure be red after you cry, because I'm gonna—"

"Stop it!" I yell, even though I'm secretly enjoying this.

They glare at each other, then slowly sit back down.

"You're right, Chloe; Rye is not Superman. He's Rye," I say. "You're not perfect either. None of us are. Not even Superman."

Chloe slumps her shoulders and lowers her eyes. I feel guilty immediately.

"You two are both amazing. It makes me incredibly happy to call you my friends. And don't worry, Chloe, you are not disinvited from our wedding."

"Ha!" says Chloe, sticking her tongue out at Rye. She never acts quite like this in high school. Change is an inevitable side effect of years, I suppose. Both good and bad.

Rye smiles.

"We should try to get along, Chloe," he says. "And maybe, someday, we can all be friends."

Chloe seems unconvinced, but she doesn't appear to be upset anymore. There in high school, Chloe is glad I have such a strong relationship with Rye. Years build strength and bonds nothing can break. There in high school, Chloe knows Rye makes me happy. So she's happy too. Here in kindergarten, she's just too young to understand. And I'm too old to question that.

We take out our lunches and eat. Two of my best friends sit by my side unknowingly. They're oblivious to my years. We talk about kindergarten things, and at times, all three of us laugh in synchrony. Together. A girl feeling uneasy about the new someone receiving her best friend's attention— one who needs to let go of the negatives to make room for the positives. A boy feeling a shifted sense of joy for his new friend, who, even though he doesn't know it, will become much more— one who has the longevity of love ahead.

And don't forget about the fool who feels lost in her own years— one who feels the pain of every ceaseless second. And when the fool hides, out comes Jessica Jule Locke with all of her pieces. But she's not home.

Sitting in the small lunchroom with my mind running wild, I feel a brush of movement against my hand. Looking down, I see a ladybug crawling on it. The ladybug remains on my skin, and for a while, I let it. It crawls around in circles, seemingly lost and disoriented. Noticing its troubles, I make my best effort to guide it back toward the floor. Then I realize that there's no point. It would be free from the confined space of my hand only to be trapped in a much larger, more confusing area. So I allow the ladybug to go about according to its wishes.

And I take a moment to think about my own.

6 years of youth

As I take a moment to think about my wish, I can only hope I'll be able to bring my high school experiences back with me to kindergarten.

When my years finally switch back, I want to get at least a little reward for all my hard work. So when I go back to kindergarten, I'll have plenty of tales to tell. How do I know, they'll ask? I have my ways with years.

I'll tell everyone that big kids get lots of homework and have no playtime. I'll tell them that, as a big kid, you have many teachers instead of just one, and they call on you even if you don't raise your hand. And they don't even use popsicle sticks! I'll tell all of the kindergarteners about TAYFABYAPA, and how everyone started yelling in the middle of class. I'll tell them about the crazy, crowded hallways, and the struggle of finding classroom after classroom

170

without a teacher to guide you. And I'll tell them I have a boyfriend, because that's just how cool the big kid me is. Maybe I'll even tell them that high school isn't so bad. Or maybe I'll just keep that to myself.

Chloe and I sit at paint-stained tables in art class. All around the room are stools with different patterns of paint. Mine is red with black dots, reminding me of a ladybug. I notice this classroom is way different than the others I've seen so far, but I think I like it. All of the art supplies and bright colors remind me of kindergarten.

A man with a serious face and a paint-stained apron stands at the front of the room.

"In tribute to today's holiday, you will all spend your class time painting with a theme. Today, your task is simple, as simple as this: compose a painting that encompasses all of what Valentine's Day means to you. It should have many meaningful symbols, as well as an intellectual message. These paintings will be displayed around the school, so please use your time wisely. You may begin."

Looking around the room, I see big kids who seem happy about the work, while others look the same way I feel when I don't get a swing at recess. One girl even starts to cry, saying Valentine's Day should be illegal.

"I'll get the stuff," says Chloe.

The teacher walks around giving everyone a large piece of paper, and I think about what I'm going to paint. In kindergarten, I love coloring, and this doesn't seem much different. I'm not sure what the teacher meant when he said we have to paint something with symbols and a message, but I think I'll be able to figure it out. Of my many challenges in high school as a six-year-old, this one shouldn't be too difficult. And I'm not too far from home.

"We got the last watercolors!" says Chloe, bringing paint, a few brushes, and a cup of water to the table. "Don't overthink this. You can basically draw whatever you want as long as you have a good explanation."

I look at the watercolors, and I feel closer to home. I've used these before in kindergarten, and seeing them again brings back memories of what seems like a long time ago, even though I know it's only been two days. This is the only high school class so far I think I'll be able to easily blend in with the big kids, the first class I won't feel like just a stupid kindergartener.

If my years are on my side, this will be my last day of high school until my teenage years are true. But if I leave, I think I'll miss this place. Ten years is a long time.

Thinking of how I've always pictured Valentine's Day, I soak a thick brush in water, then dip it into red paint. As neatly as possible, I draw a big red heart across the paper, but it turns out dull and droopy.

"That's all you can think of?" asks Chloe with a frown.

Because I know I need more detail, I dip my brush into black paint and put an "x" through the heart to show how sad parts of today have been. It shows Rye's sadness after he gave me the bracelet, it shows my sadness when I realized he was sad; it shows the sadness of being six years old in high school on Valentine's Day. To prove my point, Chloe looks at me with sad eyes.

"I'm sorry, Jess. I know today hasn't been your best, but you always have a way of making things better," she says. "And remember: me, Kayla, Kora, and Aimee are coming over after school, and we're bringing food."

For the sake of my sixteen years of youth, I dip the paintbrush in yellow to draw the sun. This time, the brush is less watery, so the sun comes out bold and bright next to the heart that has paint dripping off its sides.

"That's more like it! Maybe you should paint flowers too, like the blue tulips Rye gave you."

Using blue paint, I draw the petals of a tulip, then use green to draw the stem. It looks nothing like how it's supposed to, but I don't care. To me and my six years, it's perfect. No big kid can tell me otherwise.

When I look at Chloe's paper, I see neat red hearts and faces I don't recognize, but I'm sure the sixteen-year-old me would. Having Chloe as my best friend makes this crazy place called high school so much easier, and seeing her six years every day at kindergarten makes me happier than she'll ever know. As I think about how lucky I am, I dip my paintbrush in purple and draw two smiley faces, then use blue to draw frowny faces. You need sadness for happiness to be real. Next, I paint another smiley face with yellow, and I try my best to make it look like Rye. After that, I paint my locket, then a ladybug in the center of the paper.

After a while, my painting is complete. I look around to see that, while a few look like they were done by a professional artist, others are still mostly blank. The teacher walks around with a clipboard in his hand, and starting at the front of the room, he looks at the big kids' paintings. He shakes his head and frowns at many, and smiles at few. When he comes to the back of the room where Chloe and I sit, he stares at my painting, taking breaks to write something on his clipboard, but I don't dare look at him. I'm afraid he'll be mad at me for not having a clear message.

"Amazing," he says. "Although it's certainly not exceptionally painted, your message is clear and profound."

"Is that good?"

"It's wonderful!" says the teacher, and it seems like he's not even joking. "The faded heart with the bright sun symbolizes how we only see with clarity what is yearned. The faces of happy and sad emotions show different ways one may feel on Valentine's Day, and the small details add a sense of story. There is so much symbolism and a distinct message."

The teacher moves back to his desk at the front of the room, and most of the big kids look at me with what I think is jealousy. But there's no way a high schooler could be jealous of a kindergartener. Or maybe my years have no rules.

"You see, I knew—"

Chloe stops when we see Mindi walking toward our table, but to my surprise, Laura is nowhere in sight. Mindi smiles, but strangely, her eyes look sad.

"Hey, Jessica; hey, Chloe," she says. "Can I sit here?"

Chloe looks at me with wide eyes, but I'm far too shy to say no. I'm curious to see why she would decide to talk to us.

Mindi sits on the stool next to me, and Chloe continues to look confused. I'm confused too, but not in the same way I have been during most parts of high school. This is far stranger than Spanish class.

"I know we don't talk often," says Mindi. "Well… actually, we don't talk at all. You see, for so long now, I've been best friends with Laura, and sometimes, it feels like Laura exclusively. This is obviously no news to you, but she's awful. Like, *really* awful. All these years, I've been following her pointless bitterness and obnoxious ways, and I can't stand it any longer. I won't."

Mindi looks at the ground with sad eyes, then back at me and Chloe.

"Laura's the worst; all she does is boss me around. I've always wanted a friendship like yours. And I know this is many years too late, but I just wanted to say sorry. I'm sorry for being a part of Laura's unkind ways, and for the trouble we've caused you. I have many regrets."

The three of us are silent for a moment.

I was not expecting that. Not at all. Mindi is one of the popular ones! And she's apologizing to *us*? Maybe Mindi just doesn't follow the rules of being popular anymore, just like I don't follow the rules of age.

"That's okay, Mindi," I say. "I have regrets too. Lots of them, actually. I think we all just need to remember what Mrs. Rose always says: 'Being kind to others is just a different way of being kind to yourself.'"

For the first time I've seen, Mindi laughs what looks to me like a real, unforced laugh.

"Mrs. Rose? You mean from kindergarten?"

Oh, no. I start panicking right away, but then I realize I don't have to. My real years are who I am. They're a part of me, and a part of my true sixteen-year-old self. Even with my big kid disguise, I'm still a kindergartener. Even here in high school.

"Yes, Mrs. Rose from kindergarten," I say with relief. "She's taught me so much."

"I can barely remember anything from kindergarten," says Mindi. "Maybe it's best that way."

I don't think I could ever forget kindergarten, but I know my life will be so much different when I'm actually a big kid. Just because you don't remember something, doesn't mean it hasn't changed you.

"Well, I should finish my painting," says Mindi. "It was nice finally talking with you two."

She stands and starts to walk away, but before she can go far, Chloe stops her.

"Mindi," she says, "do you wanna sit with me and Jess at lunch tomorrow? I'm sure Laura would hate that, but I think you should."

Mindi smiles, and so does my youth.

"I would love to," she says. "Thanks."

Mindi walks back to her table, and she looks happier than I've ever seen her. Seeing her break the well-known rules of being popular makes me feel less nervous about breaking the rules of my youth. I'm sure Mindi won't be Laura's best friend anymore. And I won't let my life revolve around the so-called rules of age. My years can do anything.

The bell rings a few minutes later, and I'm free. I say goodbye to Chloe, rush through the mobs of big kids, and finally, I leave the high school for the area of grass between where I belong and where I chose to be. Then I sit and wait for my youth to come back to me.

16 years of youth

I sit cross-legged on the kindergarten floor, eager for my years to return to me.

The day almost over, Mrs. Rose sets up the final activity of my second false day of youth. No matter how pointless it is for a high school student, I'm still excited for active play. There's something soothing about sitting down and mindlessly playing board games or stacking blocks. Something I've missed.

Active play begins, and us kindergarteners move to various parts of the room. Sitting in the corner building separate stacks of blocks with Rye and Chloe, I think about what tomorrow will bring. I can say with near certainty that my six-year-old self will want to switch back permanently. I'm sure she's struggling in high school, as any kindergartener would. I'm sure she misses this place. I sure miss certain aspects of my true years. I miss Rye, Chloe, and all the positives that come with high school. I miss the challenges, I miss learning new information instead of sitting through redundant lessons. I miss having my mind in my corresponding body, my years belonging to me.

I build the blocks up to six, then accidentally bump into them, causing the tower to fall to the ground. Absentmindedly, I begin building it back up, then stop as I realize there's no point. I'll be out of kindergarten in a matter of minutes, so I better start getting used to it. I don't need to rebuild my tower.

Instead of worrying about the blocks, I just think. I think of high school and the challenges that come with it compared to the easy life at kindergarten. I think of seeing Rye again, and of what will change this Valentine's Day.

I think of my many years of youth.

6 years of youth

Just like yesterday, I know we're going to switch back. Except, this time, it could be forever, and I'll be left as a part of her memory. Today could be my last day of high school as a six-year-old, because I know my sixteen-year-old self will be eager to switch back. Even though we have barely met, I somehow know her so well.

I'm sure I could get used to high school if I stayed a little longer. It would be easy in no time. I could get used to finding classes and learning information that doesn't seem to make any sense. I could get used to talking with big kid Chloe and all of the other high schoolers, even though they're ten years older than me. And I could definitely get used to having a boyfriend. With time, I could get used to being a big kid.

But I would miss kindergarten.

I would miss talking with Chloe as her six-year-old self. I would miss recess and active play. I would miss being me. Not too long ago, I thought the hardest decision in life was choosing between chocolate ice cream or vanilla. Maybe I'm wise beyond my years.

I just can't decide. Not now, and maybe not ever, but I know I'll have to eventually. Maybe I can just pretend. If my years don't follow the rules of age, maybe time will always work differently with them.

When I look up, I see her, and I greet her with a smile. Before we can switch, my locket buzzes. A message plays out loud:

you will switch back your years for now, like yesterday / tomorrow when you meet here, you will decide which years stay

177

I look into the eyes of my sixteen-year-old self with so many different feelings I couldn't possibly describe them all. We switch lockets, the ground spins, and within seconds, we're back into our bodies that match our years. My feet are lifted up off the ground as my years walk away.

For now, I'm me again. But I don't feel as happy as I think I should.

16 years of youth

For now, I'm me again. And I'm ecstatic.

Although I do wish I didn't have to wait until tomorrow to switch back permanently, I don't mind. I'm sure my six-year-old self is just as disappointed as I am. I can't imagine what it would be like to go to high school at age six. Kindergarten is where she belongs, and where she should want to be. But now, I'll have more time to consider my years. And so will she.

As I find a seat on the bus, I think about what it will be like to see Rye again. Real Rye. It feels like forever since I've seen him, despite me saying goodbye to his kindergarten youth less than five minutes ago. It doesn't take long for me to notice a beautiful silver bracelet on my wrist, and when I do, I know it's from him. It has charms of our names, an artichoke, a swan, and a few others. It's perfect. I text him right away.

Jess: *Thank you soooo much for the charm bracelet!!! :) It is just as perfect as you are. Do you wanna come over at 4?*

I feel something unusual in the large compartment of my backpack, so I open it to find a bouquet of blue tulips. They're crushed in places due to them being squished in the bag, and I know my kindergarten self is to blame. Instantly, the flowers remind me of Rye giving me a single blue tulip at recess today, and despite the ten years' difference, the thought behind both makes me smile just the same. He knows me so well.

A few minutes later, I have one new message, but from Chloe, not Rye.

Chloe: *Hey, Jess. Did you apologize to Rye yet?*

Oh, no. Now what? Knowing my six-year-old self managed to get sulfur in her eyes yesterday has me dreading what could have gone wrong today. The actions of my youth are the responsibilities of my elder years.

Jess: *Not yet. Can you remind me what exactly I did? My memory might be different than yours.*

Chloe: *Rye gave you that expensive bracelet and flowers and you just said "thanks" and asked for chocolate and cookies. You were pretty upset after. You don't remember?!*

I officially hate this experiment. I despise my six years of youth, and I despise my sixteen. Or maybe I simply despise my decision.

Why didn't I think about Valentine's Day before I decided to spend another day in kindergarten? Maybe my years distracted me. Maybe hope lured my youth into oblivion. I'll never be able to go back to the moment I felt the need to switch my years. But then again, I never thought I would find myself back in kindergarten. I wish I hadn't returned to Mrs. Rose's classroom. As soon as I took my first step into false youth, I felt more lost than ever before. My years will never be the same, because now I know. I know everything, yet I take in little. And I change nothing. At this moment, I wish I had never wished. But only a small selection of wishes can ever truly be granted.

Jess: *I feel awful!!! Was he upset?*

Chloe: *He seemed to be. More than that, I think he was surprised. But I'm sure everything will be fine after you talk to him. You always fix any rough situation eventually! Also, do you still want me, Kayla, Kora and Aimee to come over at 3, or would a different time work better?*

I have no idea why they're coming over, but right now, I don't care. Aimee only ever speaks to me to correct my grammar, and Kayla and Kora are exceptionally nice, but we don't talk often. A lot can change in the span of a two-day switch of ten years.

Jess: *3 is fine. See you then.*

I'm about to put my phone away, then I get a new text. Looking at the screen, I see one new message from Rye, and panic quickly invades my thoughts.

Rye: *Hey, Jess. I'm glad you like it. Sorry if I got too upset with you today. And yes, I look forward to seeing you at 4.*

I hastily respond.

Jess: *No, it's completely my fault! I'm sorry I seemed ungrateful. I've been having a rough day, but I know that's no excuse. I'm sorry.*

The real reason would be a perfectly fine excuse. If only it were a reason I could tell.

Rye: *I forgive you. See you at 4.*

I put away my phone and sigh. Why did my six years of youth have to be *so* stupid? I want to tell Rye it wasn't me, but me in my wrong years. I want to tell him about the switch, because I want him to understand. I want to tell him everything, but the words of my locket hold me back.

Staring out the window, I think of all my regrets. Looking at the sky, I see the faint glow of a rainbow, but when I blink, it vanishes.

13

6 years of youth

J ust like yesterday, nothing has changed, yet everything feels

different.

Back from high school, I now relax within the walls that match my years. No wish could ever change who I am while I'm here. When I'm in this house, my years have to be true, and no matter what my age, my locket has no power over my home. It's the same as it was before the switch, but my eyes see everything differently. I no longer see life as a six-year-old.

My kindergarten days are weak compared to the rush of being a big kid.

I sit on the couch with nothing in particular to do. My parents are upstairs with my six-month-old brothers, so I feel completely alone until my eyes become attached to something I see every day. But now, it's so different.

On the counter is a framed photo of me from the day I turned a year old. My hair is a mess of light brown curls, and I wear a shirt with a pattern of endless rainbows. I hold the photo and stare at baby Jess's bright smile, which makes all of my six years smile back. I hope my high school self felt the same way when she saw me yesterday.

If my one-year-old self had the chance to switch to my years, I think she would. But I would never make that trade. She looks happy in the photo, but my smile is six times bigger. All I want is to jump ahead, because if I don't, I worry I'll be left behind. Looking into my younger eyes, I think about what she would want. But I have no way of knowing. Our years don't match.

I hear footsteps, so I look away from my memory to see my mom walking downstairs.

"Mrs. Rose says you've been doing well lately, Jess," she says. "That's so great to hear."

Mrs. Rose said that? About me? Or my false years? Maybe both have done well.

"When did she say that?" I ask. But I'm not so sure I want to know.

My mom smiles and sits next to me.

"Every time I talk with her she has wonderful things to say. She's very pleased with the work you've been doing."

Me. Six and sixteen. Me.

"And because I'm so proud of you, I got you this."

She hands me a pink, heart-shaped box.

"I've been wanting chocolate all day!" I say. "Thanks, Mom!"

"You're very welcome. Just don't eat all that candy at once. And no staying up late tonight."

Rules. My mom's are easy to follow. But no one gave me rules about my years. *No going to high school as a kindergartener. No talking with the big kid you. No switching, no tricks, no hopeless wishes.* Never have I been more thankful for simple.

I return my eyes to my single year of youth, and her future looks brighter.

16 years of youth

Once I'm home from my second day in my false years, I toss my backpack on the ground and collapse onto the couch in my calm, quiet living room. My brothers will be at a birthday party with my parents all afternoon, so I'll have no annoying kids around to bother me.

Not even kindergarten Jess.

My anxiety toward the rest of today as well as not knowing what years I'll be in tomorrow lingers in my every thought. Right now, my most prominent concern is Rye. Considering the catastrophes of the last two days, I know it will be far from perfect. But it's Valentine's Day. It has to be special.

It's now 2:30, so Chloe and the others should be here in half an hour. I'm not sure what we're going to do or why exactly they planned to come in the first place, but it doesn't matter. I don't care.

The more I think about him, the more I realize high school Rye and kindergarten Rye aren't much different, despite the many years of youth between them.

For the short time before my friends come over, I decide to sit and do nothing. The older I've gotten, the more this has become one of my favorite pastimes. After a long day of relaxation and confusion just the same, there is nothing better than sitting down and breathing. No working, no moving, no worrying. Just breathing.

***

Ding dong.

I bolt awake, all the nothingness having carried me off into sleep. Groggily, I roll off the couch and open my front door.

183

"We're here with food," says Chloe. She walks inside, followed by Kayla, Kora, and Aimee.

"Um… I do love food," I say. "What exactly did you guys plan on doing here?"

"We're going to sit, talk, and eat way too much food," says Chloe.

"Sounds good, but first, what homework do we have? I forgot to —"

"Food and talk!"

"While those two activities certainly sound pleasant, Jessica also promised she would help me with my social skills," says Aimee. "If you would *please* do that, I would very much appreciate it, and also, *thank you.*"

I can't imagine why or how my six-year-old self managed to get Aimee to ask me for help. Maybe my younger years are smarter than I thought. I think it's about time I stop referring to myself as an idiot.

"I'll help you as best I can, Aimee," I say, even though my social skills are mediocre at best. "Rye should be here at four, so you can just hang out in my room while he's here."

"Sounds like a plan," says Chloe. "What is it you're going to give him?"

"A gift," I say, wanting to keep it a secret.

"A gift of what?"

"A gift of wishes."

And despite the ambiguity, I leave it at that.

The five of us sit down on my living room couch next to a counter that holds a picture of me when I was one year old. Kayla opens a cooler and takes out a tub of chocolate ice cream, my favorite. Kora sets out sprinkles, chocolate syrup, and whipped cream, then in the tub of ice cream, we work together to create one giant sundae.

I get five large spoons from the kitchen, then hand one out to everyone. We're about to dig our spoons into the ice cream, but then —

"Wait!" says Aimee. "I brought organic dried mango. Before you ask, yes, I am very much aware of the fact that dried mango is not as nutritious as fresh mango, but I wanted to be adventurous."

Aimee opens a bag of dried mango, and we each put some on a spoonful of ice cream. Then finally, we eat. It's a strange combination of foods, but delicious just the same.

"Remember when we were younger and you would always give half your dessert at lunch to Rye?" asks Chloe out of the blue. But to me, it's not so random.

"I remember," I say, my memories of my youth both false and true. "You didn't used to like Rye, did you?"

"Well... we weren't the best of friends," says Chloe. "I guess I just didn't like how much he stole your attention from me. But I forgive him now, as long as he doesn't ever dare break your heart."

"I don't think he ever will."

"Me neither," says Chloe. "Remember in kindergarten when you two scheduled your wedding?"

"I remember it like it was yesterday," I say. Well, actually, I remember it like it was today. "We decided on December 12th."

"And you promised I would be invited, remember?"

"Of course."

"You do realize that we're only in high school, correct?" asks Aimee.

"There's nothing wrong with looking ahead."

"We only have about two and a half years of high school left before college, then the unknown. It's fun to look ahead to a brighter future," says Chloe. "We're only young for so long, you know"

The rest of the group nods, but I shake my head.

"I think youth depends on one's outlook on life, not years," I say. "Someday, when we're all old people, we could be just as young and free as we are now if we want to. Sure, we can't choose to be rich, or to be free of health problems, or to have everything we want in life. But we can choose to be happy. We can choose to be young, even when we're old."

"I mean, we would make a pretty great old people squad," says Chloe.

"Yes, yes we would," I say. "We could buy matching walking canes that play music and glow in the dark."

"And play bingo, but with lots of added twists."

"We could be young and old at the same time," I say. "But for now, we should just enjoy being teenagers."

"This tangent on what defines youth has been of minimal interest, and I do believe there was a set purpose to this get-together we have yet to address," says Aimee. "You promised you would teach me about social skills, Jessica."

"I'll teach you what I know," I say. "How about we start with greetings. We'll split this lesson into two parts: what you're doing wrong, and how you can fix it. So for greetings, I notice sometimes when you see me or someone else in the halls at school, you avoid eye contact and shake your head."

"Why is that bad?" asks Aimee. "I avoid eye contact and shake my head simply because I am utterly flabbergasted by the display of tomfoolery in the hallways, such as running, screaming, and throwing various objects. And even if I am to pass an innocent walker, my actions remain constant, as I am aware it is polite to treat everyone equally. Why would such actions imply poor manners?"

"Why don't you just smile and say hello?"

"Does one smile and say hello to the maniacal animals at a zoo?"

"Come on, Aimee, you know that's not a fair comparison," I say. "Don't you feel happy when people smile and say hello to you?"

"I feel very socially awkward in said situation."

"Then we'll work on that too. But most people are happy when people smile and say hello. It makes you seem a lot more friendly."

Aimee pauses, and she seems to be considering the idea.

"You truly suppose that will help me?"

"I truly do."

"Very well, then," says Aimee. "Let's practice. Pretend you're walking in the hall, and I'll, um... I'll smile and say hello."

"You got it," I say, and we both stand.

We walk across the room from opposite ends, then meet in the center. Aimee stops abruptly and stands still and stiff.

"Hello, Jessica!" she says with an over-exaggerated, clearly forced smile. We both sit back on the couch.

"Okay... I guess that wasn't... horrible. What are your thoughts?" I say, looking awkwardly at the group.

"Well, you said hello," says Kayla. "And you certainly smiled."

"And you made eye contact," says Kora. "So, that was good."

"Just tell me," says Aimee, frowning.

"Well, next time maybe don't completely come to a stop, but instead say hello while passing by," says Chloe. "And also, you don't need to smile quite so much. Try not to make it look fake."

"How about this?" asks Aimee, curving her lips into a smile but keeping her eyes dull.

"Just pretend I told you a funny grammar joke."

"Okay, how's this?" asks Aimee, pretending to laugh, but making no noise.

"I have an idea," I say. "When walking through the halls, you could pretend everyone has evolved to have perfect grammar! No more forgetting when to use which form of 'your.' No more mistaking 'who' for whom.'"

"And no more confusion as to when to use 'I, me, or myself?' Or the classic ignorance of how to use proper subject-verb agreement?"

"Sure!"

"That would be a whole new world!" says Aimee, her face lighting up with a genuine smile.

"There you go!" I say. "That's a good smile! All you have to do is think about good grammar, smile, and say hello to people in the hall. You'll be less socially awkward in no time!"

Aimee pretending everyone has perfect grammar may be harmless, but the way my youth lies may bring more frowns than smiles. I pretend my years are younger by going to kindergarten, and I pretend my youth was never lost. But I won't be able to pretend for long.

"That's genius!" says Aimee. "I suppose it's only logical for us to eat more ice cream now."

"I suppose it is."

We all eat more chocolate ice cream topped with mini donuts and dried mango while continuing to talk about manners. It's crazy to think about how Aimee knows more information academically than I probably ever will, but a concept as seemingly simple as smiling and saying hello is so difficult for her. I'm pretty sure I learned that in kindergarten. Real kindergarten. Six-year-old me as my six-year-old self.

But who am I to judge?

"I think that's all the social skills necessary for today," says Aimee. "Who wants to play sloth trivia?"

"Play *what*?" asks Chloe.

"Sloth trivia. Trivia of sloths."

We all agree, because why not?

"I'll ask the first question," says Aimee. "I suppose I should start easy. What is the maximum number of hours the average sloth sleeps per day?"

Nobody has any guesses.

"I'll give you a clue: it's more than the square root of 225."

"16?" asks Kayla.

"Incorrect."

"What about 17?"

"Incorrect."

"18?" asks Chloe.

"Incorrect."

"19?"

"Now you're just cluelessly moving up by a factor of one!"

"What about 21?"

"It might be a logical idea for you to move down one."

"20!" says Chloe.

"That is correct! Now you get the honor of asking the next sloth trivia question."

"Um... I don't know much about sloths, but I'll give it a go," says Chloe. "What is one thing sloths are good at?"

"Swimming!" says Aimee, hand raised. "They're horrible at running, but they sure can swim."

"Correct!" says Chloe, even though I know she has no idea.

Although sloth trivia sure is fun, I soon zone out and just think. I think about how Rye should be here soon, and my heart speeds up. Whatever my six-year-old self managed to mess up at high school today is my job to fix. I wish I could tell him. I wish I could explain why I've been acting so strange and childish at school, but I don't even know what else I've done. I wish I could tell him that the years he's been seeing at school the past few days don't represent the best me. I wish I could tell him everything. But, as I've finally come to accept, I can't.

As I think about my years, I look up at the ceiling and stare at a row of cone-shaped lights. Near the light bulbs are small clusters of red and black, dome-shaped creatures I recognize as ladybugs. A few months ago, we had a ladybug infestation in my house, and I still see a few of them here and there every so often. But there's more than just a few ladybugs inside the row of ceiling lights.

And they're all dead.

I'm not sure why they're drawn toward the light, but it's no business of mine to question. I can imagine how they feel— flying toward the light, toward what could be their own form of happiness, toward hope, but once they get there, the heat kills them. I understand.

When I wished to return to my younger years, I was a ladybug searching for light. But now that I'm back in kindergarten, I realize I don't belong, that the restrictions of my false youth are the heat of the light I can't handle. And unless my six-year-old self wants to switch back as much as I do, I'll be stuck.

In one light, I see a ladybug that's still alive, crawling closer and closer to the bulb. I want to tell it to stop, to get away. I want to tell it the light may be beautiful, but the heat that comes with it can kill. But I can't. The ladybug crawls toward the heat, then abruptly goes still. A tear rolls down my cheek as I grieve for the ladybug and fear for my own light and the heat that comes with it.

"Jess?"

I draw my eyes away from the ceiling to see my friends staring at me with quizzical eyes.

"Are you okay?" asks Chloe.

"I'm fine."

"What's wrong?"

I try to hold them in, but the tears come falling out. Everything wrong with the past two days hits me all at once. I no longer perceive my false youth as a promising light; I feel it as a burning fire. My friends move closer to comfort me in my sorrow.

"If sloth trivia is upsetting you, we may certainly replace it with another activity," says Aimee. "Yes, it is unfortunate that sloths can only climb 6-8 feet per minute, but at least they get up to 20 hours of sleep per day."

"No, it's not that."

"Is it that sloths continuously urinate in the same area, leaving them vulnerable to predators?"

"No, it's not the sloths. It's just that... it's that... *I feel like a ladybug!*"

I continue to cry as my friends look just about as confused as I would be if someone told me a week ago I would find myself back in kindergarten.

"I understand," says Aimee. "Ladybugs often find themselves in lack of food, so they resort to cannibalism. It must be awful to feel like that."

"No!" I point to the ceiling lights, but no words come out.

"Oh, I understand," says Aimee. "You're upset because ladybugs infested your house in the past, and seeing them now brings back horrific memories."

I shake my head.

"Ladybugs are cool," says Kayla.

"The coolest," says Kora. "It makes sense that you would feel like one, considering how cool you are, Jess."

"If I could be any bug in the world, I would for sure be a ladybug," says Chloe.

"Actually, ladybugs are technically beetles, not —"

"*Aimee!*"

I know they're trying to help, but their words only make me realize the fault in my youth more. And with every realization, the heat grows stronger.

"I feel like one of *those* ladybugs," I say, pointing to the ceiling lights.

"Well, they're all dead," says Aimee.

"*I know!*"

"Don't worry, Jess, you're one of the most lively people I know," says Chloe. "You'll live a long, happy life. And someday, we'll be the coolest old people around."

"No, that's not it," I say. "I feel like one of those ladybugs on the ceiling lights. Every time I try to change something, or reach for something in life that I just can't grasp, I feel like I'm going to end up like one of those ladybugs."

"You're not going to be like one of those ladybugs, Jess," says Chloe. "Present challenges make future ones easier. And if—"

Ding dong.

It's only 3:50, but Rye almost always arrives early. I glance at the ceiling lights for a moment, then turn toward my friends.

And I leave my sorrow behind to create room for happiness ahead.

"You guys should head upstairs now," I say. "I'll be fine."

"Are you sure you're okay, Jess?" asks Chloe.

Am I okay? What a complicated question in need of a simple answer. The fire of my youth has slowly beaten back into a pleasant, subtle heat, and I no longer fear a burn. But something is wrong. Something that may never truly be fixed.

"Yes."

If not now, then with just a little time.

14

<u>6 years of youth</u>

I t's so sad.

It's sad that I could decide to go to high school tomorrow and leave
the big kid me stuck in kindergarten. It's sad she lets her six-year-old
self control her, and it's sad that, until now, I didn't think it was sad
at all.

I sit in my room playing with dolls. In my left hand, I hold a
Barbie that looks about the same age as the older me I've gotten to
know. In my right, I hold a doll that looks about my age. The two are
both important to my collection, but when together, they're not fun
to play with. Their years don't match.

Looking at the younger doll, I feel a connection. I've had her for
as long as I can remember, and something about her feels like home.
But when I look at the Barbie, I feel excitement for the new, more
interesting doll. Back and forth between the two, I decide to play
with the younger doll. But as soon as I put the Barbie away, the
younger doll just isn't the same without it. So I put both away. And I
look into my mirror.

The sun shines through my window and hits my mirror in the
perfect way to make a small, shy rainbow on my cheek. It isn't in the

classic curved shape I normally see outside. Instead, it's just a blob of colors.

It's sad my sixteen-year-old self is lost. But I love her. And she'll always find me.

16 years of youth

"Why are you sad?" asks Rye. I feel my cheeks to find them still drenched in tears.

"I feel like a ladybug," I say, and he doesn't seem remotely confused by the statement. I guess he knows my weirdness so well by now that it no longer comes as a surprise. "How are you?"

"I don't know. Everything's felt different the past two days, but I don't even know what 'everything' is. Maybe it's all in my head," he says, and I immediately understand. "Also, I miss Paul."

"We saw Paul yesterday," I say, thinking of the giving swan and Paul, the smallest fish in the lake.

"Yesterday was a long time ago."

"Yesterday was less than 24 hours ago."

"Are we really going to debate the stretch of time in which one starts to miss a fish?"

"I guess not," I say. "I haven't seen you since yesterday either."

"But you saw me at school today."

Oh… right. I did see him at school today. But I wasn't there.

"Oh," I say, avoiding his gaze. "I guess I just forgot. I've felt so different at school lately. Maybe it's the stress."

Somehow, I know he understands. But at the same time, I know he couldn't possibly know.

"Thank you again for the bracelet. I'm sorry I was ungrateful at school today, but trust me when I say this is very important to me. Just like you."

"Did you like the artichoke charm?" asks Rye, laughing a little.

"I love it," I say. "The swan was also a good one."

"I'm glad," he says. "I also missed you, a lot more than Paul. You're right; you haven't been acting like yourself at school."

"I know, and I'm sorry. I've been hopelessly trying to figure out who I want to be, which only brings me further from being myself."

"You feel lost in your years?"

"Exactly."

"I know what that's like. Sometimes, I want to be young again, to go back to the days I had not a care in the world. Other days, I want to be older. I want to be done with school and on with the rest of my life. But most days, I want to be me," he says, taking my hand. "If you can be you, and I can be me, we'll be perfect."

"We will," I say. "I sometimes wish I could go back to when I was younger, or fast forward my life to a better future. But it doesn't have to be that way."

I hold my locket in the palm of one hand, and Rye's hand in the other.

"You're a part of me now. The swan's a part of me, and so is Paul. And next year, I'll have a whole new list of moments and memories that make up who I am. And that is what will make each year bright."

Rye looks into my eyes the same way I would imagine a sailor lost at sea would look at the sight of land.

"Why do you feel like a ladybug, Jess?"

"I don't. Not anymore."

"Good," he says. And I wonder how he knew. "So, what do you feel like?"

"I feel like me," I say. "This is the first time in awhile I can truly say that."

"I'm glad you feel like you," says Rye. "Because I love you."

Me? With all of my pieces? Or is something missing?

"You mean, you love *me* me, or my—"

"I love you, Jessica Jule Locke."

Me.

"I love you too," I say. "And our many years of youth."

We sit in silence, but his presence speaks a thousand words.

15

6 years of youth

"**I** think I like Rye," I say to my mom. She sits next to me in our living room, cartoons playing on the TV. "He gave me a bracelet today."

My mom tilts her head.

"He did?" she asks. "Can I see it?"

"Well... I don't have it," I say, frowning. "He didn't really give it to *me*. It's not mine."

And neither are my big kid years. My years are a rainbow, and my youth is colorblind.

"Then who did he give it to?"

"Um... a pretty girl who I think is confused," I say nervously. "I'm sure she loved it."

My mom wraps her arms around me, and I wonder whether or not she sees my sixteen years of youth in my eyes.

"Why is this girl confused?"

"She wants to be young. Or old. Actually, I think she wants both. But she has to choose. And I have to help her."

This is the first time this week my mom and I have spent this much time together without her being busy with other things. It's only the two of us. No crying brothers. No chores to be done, no worries to think about. Just me, my mom, and my real years. Maybe six is old enough. Maybe the pieces fit into place better than I thought before. And maybe— just maybe— I'll truly be home tomorrow.

"Would you want to have a friend over tomorrow after school?" asks my mom. "You haven't had a playdate here in awhile."

I nod, but after the past two days, the idea sounds a little strange. The last time I saw my best friend was two days ago, when our years matched. If I return tomorrow, I'll see her at kindergarten. If not, I have to let my years reach.

"I'll ask Chloe."

She's the only one I ever invite over. But that was when the only years I knew were my own. Now that I've met me at sixteen, my life is different, not just at school. She has changed everything. My big kid self is why kindergarten will never be the same again. I know it won't. I'm older now.

"Actually, I think I'll invite two friends," I say with pride. "Maybe three!"

Or maybe even four, like big kid Jess today.

My mom raises an eyebrow, and I wonder if she knows about my tricks.

"That's very unlike you, Jess."

"I know," I say. Never have I known myself better. "I think I have more friends now, or I will soon. I'll give it a try."

My mom smiles.

"You're very mature for your age, Jess," she says. "You become wiser every day. It's truly a gift."

16 years of youth

I give Rye his gift, which he receives with sixteen years and a smile.

My gift to him was wishes, wishes in the form of a shoe. I custom-ordered him a miniature silver statue of a shoe modeled after his favorite pair, which he's had for ages now. They barely fit him anymore, the leather has taken on an unpleasant, off-white hue, and they have holes in the soles that Mrs. Arthur complains about constantly.

I suggested he display the silver statue in his room and use it for wishes, similarly to how I use my silver locket. Anything can be a wish-granter if you give it power by lavishing hope upon it. Unlike me, Rye has already found his years. I wonder what he'll wish for.

After Rye once again wishes me a happy Valentine's Day, he has to leave, but my smile stays. Today hasn't been so bad, after all. It's clear Rye knows something has been different the past few days, but when both of us are together in our true years, nothing can make the spark of our youth die. Not even my crazy six-year-old self could ruin this day.

I walk upstairs to my room, but before I can get there, my friends run out, cheering as though I just won a race. And in a way, I think I have. Slow and steady is the only way to beat the time that ages you every ceaseless second.

"That was *so cute!*" says Chloe. "I hope you didn't mind that we were kind of eavesdropping, Jess."

"Not at all," I say. "Do you think it went well?"

"Perfect!" says Kayla. "Like, Romeo and Juliet perfect."

"But Romeo and Juliet both ended up dead after—"

"Not the point, Aimee!" says Kora. "That was so much better than earlier today, Jess. You two seem happy."

"We are," I say. Because now, my years are mine.

"Do you know what sounds fun?" asks Chloe. "We should all go ice skating to celebrate life!"

"Life sure is an event worth celebrating," I say. "I'm in."

Chloe calls her mom and asks her to drive us, because none of us can drive yet without an adult. I guess we truly are young.

We all cram into Chloe's mom's car, then we're on our way to our celebration of life. I couldn't be happier with my many years of youth.

***

I fall. Then get up. Then I fall and get back up again.

Maybe I'm not the best ice skater in the world, but there's something about being horrible at an activity that makes it that much more enjoyable. The other girls fall just as often as I do, and we all help each other back to our feet.

The ice skating rink is packed with people, most of whom are paired in twos. The couples skate across the rink gracefully, talking and laughing with linked arms. They seem so perfect, so strong, so stereotypical-movie-couple.

I hear a loud *thud* and turn around to help Aimee off the ground. She smiles what looks to me like a genuine smile, and although I can't know for sure, I don't think it's because she's thinking about good grammar. The five of us meet at one side of the rink, holding onto the edge and trying not to lose our balance.

"Is it truly logical for the five of us unskilled ice skaters to skate amongst this mass of Valentine's Day couples?" asks Aimee.

"No," I say. "But life doesn't always have to be logical."

"You mean, we can skate and fall down, then skate, then fall down again alongside all of these skilled people we are making a fool of ourselves in front of... for *fun*?"

"That's the idea."

"*Woah...*" she says, mouth agape. "And can we also get snow cones after this, even though we already had ice cream, *for fun*?"

"Yep!"

"And tomorrow at school, can we sit in different seats *for fun?*"

"You bet!"

"Even though it's socially acceptable for us to only sit in our unassigned, yet mentally assigned seats?"

"That just makes it more fun."

"This is going to be awesome!"

"This *is* going to be awesome!"

"Life is so much more exciting while lived outside your invisible boundaries," says Aimee, a glimmer in her eyes. "I suggest we skate more now, then proceed to get snow cones. You know, *for fun.*"

"Sounds like a plan."

We skate, then fall, then skate and fall some more. We continue for fifteen minutes or so, then a slow song plays overhead. The movement on the rink slows abruptly, and the previously loud atmosphere softens. Almost everyone around us is slow dancing with their partner, and we attempt to stay still, but end up slipping and sliding across the ice ungracefully. The five of us are stuck in the middle of the rink, surrounded by dancing couples.

"Well, this appears to be an awkward situation," says Aimee.

"It doesn't have to be." I say. "This could be fun if we let it."

"I suppose you're right!" she says.

Without a care, we continue sliding across the ice, barely avoiding couples. We're the only ones not slow dancing or staying put at the side of the rink, so we stand out from the "normal." Many people turn to look at us, and a few point and laugh. I'm sure the older skaters view us as "reckless teens," but I know I don't fit that label. My youth is free to roam outside the rules of age, yet restricted in its knowledge and memories. But no restriction can hold back my yearning for my true years. As we skate disorderly across the ice, making a scene as we do, I'm thankful for my years. They've all put in work to get me here.

Every last one of them.

"Happy Valentine's Day, everyone!" I yell, gliding across the ice. The people around us cheer, making way for us to zoom past them.

"I never would have thought I would take part in such shenanigans!" says Aimee.

"See, if you just—"

I fall mid-sentence, then the other four crash in after me. We all laugh, look around to see a room full of strangers laughing with us, then laugh some more. Random skaters help us to our feet, and we walk back over to the edge of the rink.

"I think that's enough ice skating for one day," says Chloe.

"I completely and utterly agree with you," says Aimee.

"Do you think we should get snow cones now?"

"That sounds like a logical thing to do."

The five of us leave the rink, take off our ice skates, and walk over to the food court.

"What can I get for you girls today?" asks the man at the snow cone stand.

"We'll have five snow cones, please," I say.

"What kind?"

"Surprise us."

"Interesting choice."

We watch him make five different snow cones, then place them on a tray patterned with rainbows.

"That will be $15.00," he says.

I give him a twenty and let him keep the change, then the five of us sit at a circular booth next to the ice rink.

"I know of a logical way to do this," says Aimee. "We close our eyes, spin the tray, and take one at random."

"Sounds like a plan," says Chloe. "I hope I get the blue and pink one."

"I want the green and red," says Kayla.

"I'm hoping for the orange one," says Kora.

"May the odds be ever in your *flavor*."

We all close our eyes, spin the tray, and grab a flavored chunk of ice at random. We then open our eyes to see who got what.

Chloe has the one Kora wanted, Kora holds the flavor preferred by Kayla, and Kayla has Chloe's choice. Aimee has an orange and yellow snow cone, and I hold a green and purple one.

"Well," says Chloe. "Maybe if we just make a quick switcheroo —"

Chloe, Kayla, and Kora make switches between the three of them before Chloe can even finish the sentence.

"You know," says Aimee, looking at me. "It might only be logical for us to switch flavors as well, considering the fact that—"

"Let's switch," I say, and we do so.

"Thanks," says Aimee. "I've never enjoyed lemon."

"I understand," I say. "I've never liked grape, so it works out."

"If only life were that simplistic," says Aimee.

"If only we could make a quick switcheroo from all the bad things in life to the good," I say. "Of our many problems as teenagers, snow cone flavors are one of the least significant."

"I completely and utterly agree with you," says Aimee. "And there's many, many more to come."

"Responsibilities."

"Uncontrollable climate change."

"Career choice."

"People who say 'who' when it is grammatically correct to say 'whom.'"

"Taxes."

"Crucial life decisions."

"Life," I say, thinking of the unknown future.

"And what about—"

"Let's not think about it now," I say. "We should eat our snow cones before they melt."

***

It's 11:58 pm, and it's still Valentine's Day. Lying awake in bed, I think about today and wonder about tomorrow.

Today was interesting, to say the least. Seeing six-year-old Rye in kindergarten and again as his sixteen-year-old self sure is an experience like no other. Of my many years of youth, I can now say with confidence that kindergarten was not the brightest. And tomorrow, if my years agree, I'll get my light back.

It's 11:59 pm, and it's still Valentine's Day. Rye said he loves me. *Me*. Sixteen-year-old Jess as sixteen-year-old Jess. I'm sure he wonders why the girl he loves hasn't been in high school the last couple of days. I wonder if six-year-old Rye has noticed a difference between me and my kindergarten self. My guess would be that his youth was oblivious to my false years. He is only in kindergarten, after all. But "only in kindergarten" will never sound the same.

It's midnight, and it's February 15. Today is the day I'll finally be me again. So long as my six-year-old self agrees to switch back, as I'm sure she will, I'll be me. I'll walk through the halls of the high school where I belong. I'll buy soft drinks from the school vending machine instead of sipping on juice boxes. I'll be back in high school classes with my high school classmates. Rye will see the real me again in school. I'll have more TAYFABYAPA instances, more challenging classwork.

Sometimes, there's nothing better than much-needed stress. It's only been two days, but it feels like an eternity since I was in high school. Maybe that's because it's been so long since I've been truly content with my years. Until now, I never would have imagined the stresses of high school would become a mental necessity. And of my many years of youth, I never would have imagined this one could be considered the brightest. But it's not the number that makes the year; it's the adventures. And it's not the craziness that makes the adventure; it's my forever-lasting youth.

It's two past twelve and it's time for me to live. As I close my eyes and fall asleep, I see a storm of colors.

6 years of youth

It's 8:02 and it's time for me to go to bed. But I can't fall asleep.

Every time I close my eyes, I see a black and white rainbow take over the sky. At one end, I see me. My mind, my body, my years. On the other, I see an old woman. She looks at the sky with sad eyes, then looks at me and tries to get me to come closer. I won't move. I won't even look at her.

I open my eyes and leave my vision. Looking around my room, I see the box of dolls is neatly organized, except for the youngest girl doll that sits on the floor. I close my eyes again and see myself and the old woman. This time, the black and white rainbow is gone. The sky is a beautiful shade of blue, and the sun is bright and welcoming. The old woman and I sit a thousand miles apart. In the distance between us are all my years, each with their own little rainbow of the most beautiful colors.

16

16 years of youth

I t's 6:30am and, I burned my toaster waffles. There's only one

sip of orange juice left in the bottle, and I just broke a nail. But today, I get the chance to go to high school again. So all is well.

I trust that my six years of youth will want to switch back this morning when we meet. Although I haven't been her in ten years, I know her like no other. She won't want to continue high school as a kindergartner, because who would? It's like taking a test on material you've never before studied; you're consigned to failure.

After I apply a band-aid around my broken, bloody nail, eat my burnt waffles, and sip my single sip of orange juice, I walk into my bathroom and stare at my reflection. My naturally frizzy, curly hair sits in a messy bun at the top of my head with several strands breaking free and falling against my face. I take out the bun and heat up my straightening iron. My curly hair reminds me too much of my kindergarten days.

Staring into the mirror, I think about how different I look now compared to just a couple of years ago. From curly hair to only slightly wavy, to getting my braces off, to totally changing my overall style— my whole look barely resembles what it did not too long ago. I'm not sure how my six years of youth recognized me this

Tuesday morning when I was sitting on the bench, mindlessly gazing out the window. Maybe she just knew.

Once my hair is pin-straight and silky smooth, I give it a few light, delicate curls, then look into the mirror once more and sigh. It's one of *those* mornings. One of those mornings my back feels bent and my face looks like the "before" in before and after photos. One of those morning something just doesn't feel right. One of those mornings my world is askew.

My hair smelling like toxic fruit salad, I grab my navy-blue backpack and walk the half mile to the bus stop. The bus appears while I'm still fifty yards away, so I have to sprint to catch it.

I reluctantly sit with Laura in one of two remaining seats. Normally, I would ask the rhetorical question "may I sit with you?" — but it's Laura. No explanation needed.

She turns toward me and smiles, but it's not genuine or benevolent. It's the smile that means I've just landed in her trap, sort of like the smile villains make in movies before they kill their victim.

From the back of the bus, I see Mindi sitting with a girl I don't recognize, and I briefly wonder why she's not with Laura. For as long as I've known them, the two have been practically inseparable.

I look at Laura and realize some people never change. But most do. Almost everyone I've gotten to know over time has grown for the better because of their years. So I smile at Laura with hope for her sake.

"Hey, Jessica," she says. "Are you excited for English class today? We're reading more *Romeo and Juliet*, but try not to cry this time."

"Oh, I'm ecstatic," I say, looking forward to a class that doesn't involve learning what two plus two equals. "Today is going to be wonderful."

"Okay…" she says. "How did Valentine's Day go with that boyfriend of yours? I heard he gave you an expensive bracelet and you said, 'Thanks. Now where's my chocolate?'"

She laughs obnoxiously, and I cringe at the thought of my six years of youth receiving the bracelet from Rye, even though I know the moment is in my past now. I know I can't change what happened. My six years of youth is who she is. And she's a part of who I am.

"It went great, actually. I'm wearing the bracelet now," I say, showing her my wrist. "How did your Valentine's Day go, Laura?"

"*It went great, actually*," she says, horribly mocking my voice. "I got these expensive diamond earrings that probably cost three times the price of that skimpy little bracelet of yours."

She points to her ears, and the diamonds glimmer in the rising sun.

"Who gave them to you?"

"They were… *oh, shut up!*" she says, crossing her arms and turning away from me. It reminds me of how she behaves in kindergarten.

"Alright," I say. She stays silent for a few moments, but with Laura, that only ever lasts so long.

"I think I saw my grandmother wear a shirt just like that the other day," she says, referring to the pink and navy-blue short-sleeved flannel I'm wearing.

"Thanks! I like your shirt too."

"You're such an idiot."

"Your hair looks nice today."

"I *really* want to slap you in the face right now."

"I *really* want to give you a high five and wish you the best for today," I say, holding out my hand for a high five, knowing she'll leave me hanging. After a few seconds, I take my other hand and high five myself.

"I feel so bad for Rye," she says, shaking her head.

"Me too. He got a B on his English essay last week, but I think he totally deserved an A."

"I mean—"

"I know exactly what you meant," I say. Then I smile. "I like your outfit today."

Laura frowns.

"Are you doing this on purpose?"

"Yes. Kill 'em with kindness before they can make a dent on you with their words. You might want to remember that, Laura."

We're both silent for the rest of the bus ride.

***

I hop off the bus and bolt toward the grass between the high school and kindergarten. Eagerly, I push past the teenagers around me, because I just can't wait. My six years of youth is nowhere in sight, so I sit on the grass. My locket buzzes, and I open it impatiently. There's a small piece of folded paper inside, which I promptly unfold. It says:

today you and your six years of youth may talk / I hope her decision doesn't come as a shock / this experiment will always be one with lessons to remember, no matter the outcome / over the past few days, it is to your benefit that you've learned some

I refold the paper and put it in my backpack. Then I look up to see my youth staring at me.

"Hi," she says, tapping her foot nervously. How peculiar it is to be nervous to talk to yourself.

"Hello," I say. "Um... how's your life going?"

"Good," she says. She glances at the kindergarten, then the high school, and back at me. "High school's kinda difficult."

"Trust me, I know," I say, standing up. "Kindergarten's boring. Well, at least for a sixteen-year-old."

"High school sure is interesting," says my six years of youth. "Do you wanna hear something crazy?"

"Go ahead."

"You're *dating* Rye!"

"Trust me, *I know*," I say. "It seems like you and Rye had a connection even back in kindergarten. He gave me a cookie at lunch. Well, more like he gave it to you. Or, at least he thought he did."

"I'm sorry I made him sad yesterday," she says, finally stabilizing eye contact with me. "Will you tell him that?"

"I did, and we've been forgiven. I'm sorry I got you in a little trouble with Mrs. Rose. I was put in the time-out chair yesterday."

"*Woah!*" she says. "What did you do?"

"You'll find out later... I'm sure it'll be fine."

For a moment, we stare at each other in awkward silence.

"I think Rye's my favorite part of high school," says my kindergarten self, a glimmer in her eyes. "You see, he has a really nice face, and he doesn't talk to me much in kindergarten, but in high school—"

"*You devious little pint-sized Jessica!*" I say. "You can wait until you've got your own years and have him as a boyfriend of your own."

"But kindergarten Rye doesn't talk to me nearly as much as high school Rye does."

"Maybe he didn't before, but he does now."

"Really?"

I smile. "You'll see."

My youth frowns. "Do you think I'm ugly?"

"Ugly? What... why—"

"Just tell me."

"I think you're beautiful," I tell my six years, and for a second, I think I see tears in her eyes. My eyes. Our eyes.

"What about your birthmark... my birthmark? *Our* birthmark."

"I think it's beautiful. Chloe says—"

"It looks like a giraffe. I know."

"But in a good way."

"*I know!* I'm not as stupid as you think. I know you... I am you."

My kindergarten self narrows her misty green eyes and hops up on her tiptoes to scrutinize my left cheek.

"Then why—"

"Jess, listen to me, when I was truly you—"

"No! Let me finish. You know what Mrs. Rose says about interrupting."

Her lips quiver as she wipes a tear from her lightly freckled cheek.

"Why do you cover it then? If my birthmark is beautiful, why do you hide it?"

"Because I'm insecure," I tell my youth, voice shaking. "Do you know what that means?"

She shakes her head.

"It means I worry about what other people think of me. How I look, how I act, how smart I am. That's why I cover the birthmark. It's beautiful, and I never used to worry about how others saw it until I was a year or two older than you. But I can change that. We can change that. It doesn't have to be that way."

I take out a makeup wipe from my backpack. Chloe and I carry them around everywhere in case unanticipated tears smear our mascara, and the two of us have been late to many classes throughout high school due to touching up our makeup in front of bathroom mirrors. But it doesn't have to be that way.

Sliding the makeup wipe over my lightly freckled skin, I lock eyes with my youth. I smear off my mascara, my lipgloss, my concealer— all of it. My hands quiver, but my breath is steady. Secure.

My kindergarten self peers up at me with bright, beaming eyes.

"Your birthmark. *Our* birthmark. I can see it."

She glides her hand over her left cheek, her smile radiating from her face. I mirror her movements.

"You're beautiful," I tell her. Me. Us. "I love you."

6 years of youth

As a big kid, Rye sits next to me whenever he gets the chance. He gave me flowers, a bracelet, and more smiles than I can count. As a big kid, Rye likes me. But I know he likes the real sixteen-year-old me better.

I know we should switch. I really do. I don't understand a thing in high school, and recess, stickers, and juice boxes don't come with being a big kid. Talking with the kindergarten version of Chloe is another part I miss, because big kid Chloe just doesn't seem to understand me as well. I even miss kindergarten Aimee.

My real years are easier than high school, but high school is more interesting than kindergarten. So how do I choose?

I remember what my locket said on the first day of the switch: *"you may not forever return, or fix this trick in the slightest / until you decide that of your many years of youth, yours have been the brightest."* But the thing is, of my many years of youth, I don't know if mine have been the brightest. I have no way of knowing which one will be best, and I have no way of knowing if my brightest years will be true or another trick. I've only been sixteen for two school days, and I've never been an adult or an old woman. My little brothers must love being only six months old. The twins have it easy. Jacob and Jerry never have to do any work, but I don't think their lives are interesting— not nearly as much as mine, to say the least.

I'm different than most six-year-olds. I'm different than most people.

So how should I know? Well, I think I have to look at this the same way I looked at those math problems in high school: I don't know. I can't.

"School starts soon," says my sixteen years of youth. "It's time."

If we switch back forever, I'll be back in boring old kindergarten. I'll be back with six-year-old Rye who doesn't even like me that much. I'll be back with my years.

But the thing is, I don't think that matters. I haven't been sixteen yet, not truly. Kindergarten has been the best of the years I've lived as me, and those are the ones that count. I want to stay in high school, stay with big kid Rye, and be grown up. But I'm not. My wish to grow up will only come true with time. After all, if you put wings on a rock, does that make it a bird?

I look at my sixteen years of youth and smile. I love her. And I'll be her someday.

"Yes."

"*Yes?*"

"Yes. I want to be back in my own years."

"Me too," she says. "And don't worry, Rye likes you a lot. Kindergarten Rye likes you a lot more than he does me."

"Really?"

"Really. And trust me, school will get more interesting as you go along. You'll do great. I know you will."

"How do you know that?" I ask, questioning myself.

"Because I'm here today, and I'm doing just fine. So you must have done something right," she says, and I think she means it. "This has all been so confusing."

"Yes, it has," I say. "And it all started with a wish."

"I'm glad we had this experience," she says. "I've learned a lot from it."

"Me too," I say. A part of me never wants it to end. A bigger part of me needs my true years. But I'm scared of being left behind. "Once we switch back, will I just be another year of your memory?"

"No," says my sixteen years of youth. "You'll be much more than that. These past few days, you've been like a younger sister to me. You've taught me so much about myself. Thank you."

"You're welcome," I say. "Well... I guess we should switch now."

She hesitates for a moment, then nods.

"Yes, we should."

We look at each other in silence for a moment, then our lockets buzz. We open them, but this time, there is no paper. Instead, the familiar voice speaks:

I hope you have learned to never doubt in the slightest / that of your many years of youth, yours have been the brightest / to return to your years, you must make the wish / I hope this lesson is something you will forever cherish

"You'll always be an important part of me," says my sixteen years of youth. "Let's make that wish."

I take a deep breath.

"Are you ready?" she asks.

"Yes."

We look each other in the eyes and share mirroring smiles.

"3, 2, 1..."

"I wish to forever be me again."

I feel the world shake as my feet are lifted off the ground. Effortlessly, I float up into the mind of my sixteen years of youth.

Then everything is still, yet filled with life. And suddenly, I'm a kindergartener. I'm home.

My Many Years of Youth

I'm home. Yet I feel terribly lost.

I feel as though a part of me has returned and left at the same time. Grasping the locket around my neck, I ponder upon how my six years of youth's presence fills me with contentment. And I wonder why her absence gives me grief.

It's not as though her existence is new. She's been here with me ever since I was her. All of my years are with me in the form of memories, knowledge, and an everlasting voice of reason. And I'll always be with them.

I don't think many people realize just how valuable their years are. Each one has something great, and something horrible. Every year I've lived is a part of who I am today. It's unnerving to think about how different I could be if I took one away. If my six years of youth vanished, I would be unaccepting of myself. And I'm certain that this year will be an important one for my future. My many years of youth are like a puzzle; if one piece goes missing, I would no longer be complete.

It's true that some years are better than others. Everything in life has the good and the bad. But without bad experiences, how could we appreciate the good ones? So it is today, February 15, that I have truly come to realize that of my many years of youth, each one has been the brightest in its own special ways. And in other aspects, many are filled with darkness. My future is built on the inevitable highs and lows of every ceaseless second.

I step toward the high school with a mind full of hopes. Then I walk inside with a head full of wishes. And suddenly, I'm a high schooler.

17

Everything is the same, yet strikingly different. I'm seeing what I've never noticed before, but that doesn't mean it wasn't there. The only aspect of high school that has changed is my perspective. A girl who has only ever seen a single flower will visit a magnificent garden and return to her flower with a revolutionized philosophy. Yet the flower remains as it was.

Sauntering through the hallways at a slower pace than necessary, I notice a display of paintings on the wall. My eyes are drawn to one that has a dull red heart with an "x" through it, several happy faces, a few sad, and, most prominently, a ladybug next to a locket. It appears to be made by someone who felt lost, an indecisive soul who longed to understand more and wonder less. I know who made it. I know her very well.

As I arrive at my block-one high school class, I feel as though it is my first day. My second class goes the same way. By the third, my years feel a fresh sense of ease with their altered view. Everything has changed. Yet nothing is new.

***

I make it to my block-four English classroom seconds before the bell rings, yet the teacher still isn't here. Chloe, Aimee, Kayla, and Kora sit in a cluster toward the front of the classroom. It's normally set up in neat rows, but today, the entire arrangement is out of order. I walk toward the girls, and they greet me with smiles. My true youth smiles back with all sixteen years.

"Hey, Jess!" says Chloe. "We moved all the desks around!"

Looking at my friends, I now only see them as their high school selves. It wasn't something I had ever considered before, yet, after experiencing false years, it's one of the first details I notice as me. This is the most genuine Jessica I could be, and I am forever thankful.

"We're sitting outside the range of our unassigned, yet mentally assigned seats!" says Aimee. "We're messing everything up!"

For the past two weeks, Chloe's had an assigned seat as a consequence for talking too much in class. This hasn't stopped her from trying to sit elsewhere most days, because she's never been one to follow the rules. I guess I haven't either. The rules of age were made for courageous, timeless souls to break them.

I peer around the comfortingly familiar room to see our classmates staring at us with sour expressions, which I return with a nonchalant shrug and a smile.

"We saved you a seat," says Kora, pointing to a desk in the middle of the cluster.

"Thanks," I say. "I wonder why Ms. G. isn't here yet."

Ms. G.— not Mrs. Rose. Finally.

"If she doesn't come within the first fifteen minutes of class, we're allowed to leave," says Kora.

"That would be wonderful," says Kayla. "I'd love to leave high school."

"That rule only applies in college," says Aimee. "Only when leaving a lesson would be impractical and inconvenient to presumably stressed university individuals."

"That's stupid," says Chloe. "Anyways, here she comes."

Ms. G. hustles into the room with a large cup of coffee and papers in one hand, and an disorganized handbag in the other.

"She looks discombobulated," whispers Aimee.

"I apologize for my tardiness," says Ms. G. "I was— *woah...*"

She pauses and slowly looks around the classroom.

"You're all in different seats today."

Many of our peers point our way as though we have committed some sort of crime. I suppose unexpectedly changing the seating arrangement might be seen as a social crime in high school, a world where every detail feels crucial. Just wait until they get out into the real world.

"It was *them!*" says Laura, pointing at us. "Aimee sat in my seat, then Chloe, Kayla, Kora, and Jessica sat in Mindi, Chelsea, Bella, and Molly's seats, so I sat over here in Justin's seat, and Chelsea and Annie sat in Andrew and Jack's seats, and then there was no more room in this cluster over here, so the rest of the class sat in that cluster over there, and now I'm all the way over here, and *Mindi's all the way over there!*"

She reaches her hand out to Mindi, who sits on the other side of the room with a blank expression. As soon as we make eye contact, Mindi flashes a genuine smile. Even if Laura doesn't know it yet, I can tell Mindi's glad to finally be free from her grasp. And I'm glad to finally be free from my blinded view of youth.

"Grow up," says Ms. G. "You teenagers have only had to face a handful of the problems in high school that you will in the real world. I'm sure you can deal with sitting in different seats."

Laura crosses her arms and shakes her head, and my friends and I try not to laugh, but to no avail. Even Mindi snickers a little. Laura looks at us and scowls. Sometimes, I feel like she hasn't grown a day since kindergarten.

"Today, we are going to continue our reading of Shakespeare's masterpiece, *Romeo and Juliet.*"

Most of the class sighs, but I'm filled with joy. My pointlessly easy lessons in kindergarten allow me to finally appreciate high school learning.

I reach into my backpack and take out the play of two lovers. Although the switch was only for two school days, it feels strange reaching into my own bag instead of the pink butterfly one that belongs to my six-year-old self. Of my many years of youth, it is only this one I have been able to appreciate the little things that come with age so much.

"Who would care to read Juliet's first monologue?" asks Ms G.

In the midst of my sudden appreciation for my years, my hand goes up without a hint of hesitancy. I look around the room to see I'm the only volunteer.

"*Wow*, Jessica," she says Ms. G, raising an eyebrow. "It's not very often you volunteer to read."

"It's not very often I get the chance to do the things I don't very often do," I say, thinking of the past few days.

"That's certainly one way to think about it," she says. "You may begin."

I glance over at my friends. Then I read aloud along with all the voice cracks and stutters that come with my imperfect perfection.

And I'm home.

***

Rye visits me after school. We had no plans. He just came.

We sit at my dining room table building sculptures with my brothers' Play-Doh. It's good to be young. And it's good to be old.

"I made you this swan," says Rye, handing me a blue, swan-shaped piece of Play-Doh.

"I assembled this lump of Play-Doh that probably has some deep, unknown meaning for you," I say giving him a blob of every available color mixed together.

"Thanks," he says, laughing. "It kind of looks like— nevermind, it doesn't really look like anything."

"This Play-Doh swan looks like a swan," I say. "You know, if it wasn't bright blue."

"There's actually so much to be seen in this lump of Play-Doh," he says, scrutinizing the blob of colors. "If you use your imagination, you can kind of see a giant, misshapen marble."

"Or a unique, colorful rock."

"It could be strange pizza dough," says Rye. "Only your imagination knows."

"Now that we're talking about pizza dough, I'm hungry," I say. "Do you know what we should do?"

"Make food?"

"Yes! Let's make artichoke dip from the artichoke you gave me on Tuesday."

"Can we put cheese in it?"

"Of course."

I assemble all the ingredients I think might be useful, including a can of seasoned artichoke hearts to go along with the fresh one. Rye takes the artichoke he gave me out of my fridge, and I set up an assortment of kitchen tools. We stare at the gigantic pile of ingredients and tools, then at each other.

"How in the name of artichoke dip are we going to do this?" asks Rye.

"I have no idea," I say. "But I'm sure the internet knows."

We go online and find what claims to be the best artichoke dip recipe ever. Then we craft our own version, because we can. Never in my many years of youth have I been so thankful for strange plants and good company.

**

Later in the day, we visit our little dock, and later in my youth, I hope to maintain our habit of making memories here. We sit with our feet dangling over the water. The sky is clear with the exception of a few dark, lurking clouds, and the lake is calm and still.

"Do you wanna hear a knock-knock joke?" asks Rye.

"Of course I do."

"Close your eyes."

Although I'm confused as to why a knock-knock joke would involve my lack of vision, I trust him. I hear him open the backpack he brought with him, and my curiosity grows.

"Open your eyes."

Upon doing so, I see a small wooden door standing on the dock with Rye crouched behind it.

"Knock, knock."

"Who's there?"

He slowly opens the door to reveal his face. A bright red, 3D question mark is in his hands, and his eyes are lit with exuberance.

"Your future prom date?" he asks, handing me the question mark.

"Your future prom date *who?*"

"Your future prom date who will tell you lame knock-knock jokes every day as long as humanly possible," he says, and his years look determined to never weaken.

"That is the best knock knock joke I have ever heard," I say, laughing. "And yes. You will make a great future prom date."

"Thank you," he says. "Even though we're only sophomores, I thought I'd ask you now. I just couldn't wait. And by the way, the question mark is made of chocolate."

"I do love chocolate," I say. And I have no doubt my seventeen years of youth will love prom.

"I'm excited for next year," says Rye. "We should come here more often. I like this little dock."

"Me too," I say, appreciating my surroundings. "Do you want to hear something I've come to realize?"

"I would love to."

"You know how I wear this locket around my neck every day?"

I hold the locket in the palm of my hand, and he nods.

"Your mother gave it to you, right?"

"Yes. And every day for years now, I've used it to make one wish. I'm not sure if it works, and I know it sounds stupid. Some days, I make trivial wishes, and others, I wish for the unimaginable. I remember wishing for direction when I felt lost in life, and for happiness when I was sad. And often, I wish for reassurance and for hope when all seems lost. These past few days, I've realized I don't need to anymore. That's not to say I have everything; I certainly don't. But I know that many wishes will come true with my years. And many more will die. I can finally accept that. And a lot of it is thanks to you."

Rye looks at me with those eyes telling me that even when I make no sense, he understands.

"I'm glad," he says. "Are you still going to wear your locket every day?"

Looking at the sky, I see the faint glow of a rainbow, but when I blink, it vanishes.

"Yes," I say, because I wouldn't be me without my past wishes. "But today, I've decided I am never again going to open it."

As soon as the words leave my mouth, my locket buzzes. At first, I'm afraid Rye can tell. But I know he can't. Instinctively, I reach to open it, then stop abruptly. I've just made a promise. I've made a promise to me and my many years of youth to come that I will never again open my locket. It will be difficult; I know it will. Some days, opening my locket and making my one wish was all that kept me going. But I can't keep lying to myself. I won't.

"I'm proud of you," says Rye, taking my small, trembling hand in his. "I know this is difficult for you."

"It's a lot easier with you here."

The breeze creates small waves atop the lake.

"You're strong, Jess. You don't need any more wishes."

"Of my many challenges throughout my sixteen short years, nothing has ever been as difficult as letting go," I say. "I've known for awhile now that someday I'd have to give up on my fictitious wishes I've been asking this locket to grant me for so long. But I never imagined it being this much of a challenge."

"And never could I have imagined being with someone so strong, kind, and beautiful," he says, his voice steady. "But look at me now."

I turn my head to face him, and despite my sorrow, I smile.

"I think this will be a good thing," I say. "I've come to learn that all the hoping in the world won't compare to a little action when trying to make a wish come true."

"I hope we can grant wishes together someday," he says. "And I hope you find your years."

A ladybug crawls across the dock, but when I blink, it vanishes.

"And remember, Jess," says Rye, holding my hand tighter. "Our youth is young."

We stare out into the distance with a perfect silence roaming between us. I sit with one hand in his, the other clenched around my locket. My heart is with my years, my mind is pondering upon my future.

And I take a moment to appreciate the existential blossoming of the little girl who dwells in my youth.

18

86 years of youth

Gingerly, I rise from my rocking chair and grip my neon-

pink, glow-in-the-dark walking cane. Without a second thought, I put on shoes and a jacket, then leave our house for the midday beauties of California.

The air is only slightly chilly, yet the occasional gust of wind is harsh against my old, wrinkled skin. I saunter down the sidewalk without a determined destination, the purpose laying in distracting my grieving mind.

This neighborhood is where I've lived all my years; my parents' house is only a few miles away. The palm trees offer a generic image of paradise, yet the way they tower over my body sends a shiver down my crooked spine. The vast ocean is peaceful on the horizon, yet I've never felt a connection with its scenery. The sun shines proudly in the clear, blue sky, yet I view nothing as bright.

Rye and I strolled down this sidewalk not too long ago, back when every moment was filled with light. We talked about the most pointless things. He told me a joke I can no longer remember, and we laughed with the joy of two souls I dared to believe were forever young. We were happier than happiness itself, because it wasn't just happiness; it was the durability, strength, and longevity of our love.

Sometimes, I feel as though happiness only exists when sorrow is hiding.

The day before Rye's death, my mind was full of bliss for not knowing what Valentine's Day would bring. There's always something to be sad about. There always has been, and there always will be. Despite this permanent reality, I'm not always sad. Only when the joys of life are in the dark do the depths of despair take control.

I had no such control when his years were stolen with an unjust proclamation of broken eternity. Forever is a fire to time's unwished well of water— a vigorous heat that toils until the spark is old, and ice overrules the burning promise with bitter cold. As the youth left his eyes, I saw my ancient, withered reflection in his corneas. The visage plastered with many layers of lost years had the unsettling appearance of a perturbed, foreign elder. A different Jessica reflected back at me. Unexpectedly, every memory I possessed turned against me. Every decade made a hasty leap for revenge. In my eyes, I saw two figures: a princess and a monster. The former was fragile, and the latter was overbearing. Neither were me. Not my mind, not my body, not my years. Nothing was mine.

Walking aimlessly, I barely notice the pathway to the little dock on the lake. It's the one Rye and I used to go to when we were so young it pains me to think of. My years tell me to walk away, but my legs carry me farther.

I make my way down the dirt path that used to be bordered in blossoming vegetation. As soon as I'm close enough to it, I'm taken aback by what our dock has become. The once smooth, shiny wood is now chipped and uneven. The grass that seemed forever green now appears dull and withered, and the atmosphere lacks the jubilance of youth we once adored.

No ladybugs dwell here.

I take a few steps onto the dock, and the entire platform shakes, so I sit to avoid losing my balance. Everything is different. Everything is old.

My feet dangling over the edge, I look out into the curiously still lake. My eyes soon fall upon a lonely creature. A swan swims in a distrait manner, seemingly as lost and out of place as I feel in my years. The swan glances at the sky, then into the placid water. I will not dare look into the troubled creature's eyes, for I fear my own reflection will taunt me.

If our love thrived for decade after decade, shouldn't my heartbreak exist for the equivalent? The extent to which the poison of a goodbye lingers depends upon the amplitude of love for whom the farewell is given. And time is life's catalyst for suffering. A friend known for weeks will pass with just a hint of sorrow, but a companion known for many years will leave a persistent pain that will only heal entirely in synchrony to time's cruelty. The death of my dear Rye has arrived at my most inopportune moment.

With the obedience of time, my body's trembling ceases, and my screaming thoughts soften into a whisper. Then I let out a grievous sob. All my emotions are freed at once, making them that much more unbearable. I cry faster than I can wipe the tears away. I cry for Rye and his many years of youth. I cry for our memories, which will inevitably become lost. I cry simply because I'm an 86-year-old woman crying on a dock she used to visit during her good days. Then I cry more.

Then I stop. Feeling sadness only encourages its presence.

I clench the locket around my neck and sigh. I haven't opened it in seven decades. The reason I've been so averse to doing so it is unclear to me, yet I know there is a reason, a reason I can't grasp within my memory.

A recollection arrives: the wishes. I remember with clarity the daily ritual of opening my locket at times I had one wish, one hope, and one necessity. What I could have possibly needed to wish for back then is a mystery. However, I know what I would wish for now. Oh, how I know.

My fragile, wrinkled hands grasp my heart-shaped, silver locket. And without a second thought, I open it. To my dismay, a small, folded piece of paper dwells inside. I unfold it to find a message written in ancient blue ink. My eyes are old and weak, yet somehow, I'm able to read it.

Of my many years of youth, every single one of them spent with you has been the brightest in its own exceptional way. One precious Valentine's day, you gave me a wish-granter. My only request was the power to someday wish you a final farewell. I hope you feel loved in all your youth. And I hope you find your years.

I fold the piece of paper and place it carefully in my pocket. Then I close my locket and hold it in the palm of my hand. And I wonder how he knew.

I toss my wishes into the water and watch them sink.

Looking at the sky, I see the faint glow of a rainbow. With every ceaseless second, the colors flourish.

I look out into the distance in company with an overpowering silence. With one hand placed on my heart, the other on the dock for balance, I grieve for Rye one last time. Then I allow my many years with him to transform into what they truly are: an abundance of bright memories with the occasional hovering cloud of sorrow. Nothing in life is truly perfect; life perfectly bears that truth. My heart is with my years, my mind is pondering upon my future— and I smile. Of my many years of youth, this one hasn't been the brightest. Neither have any of them. That's not how you measure memories. One can't simply look at a year in their life and declare it superior. It would be like picking a favorite flower out of a planet full of gardens. All of my years together as one collective entity are what I'm comprised of, not just the bright memories selected from a blissful few. I am the creation of my many years of youth. The good years are the building blocks, the bad years the glue.

All of my many years of youth have come together to construct a captivatingly beautiful, yet frighteningly flawed creature by the name of Jessica Jule Locke.

And I barely know her.

Acknowledgments

I began writing "Of My Many Years of Youth" the morning of

Saturday, October 17, 2015. A freshman in high school, I had no clue how to write a novel; however, I had a keen desire to do so. Although my progress was slow and my lack of self-confidence led to several hiatuses, my dad, Paul McNamara, always encouraged me to continue, and for that I am so grateful. I thank my brothers, Grant and Max McNamara, for their love and support throughout our 17 years of youth.

I would like to thank my editor, John Rickards, for his patience and diligence, and for treating me like an established writer rather than a clueless high school student. Credit also goes to John Gallant, a longtime friend of my father's and the first person to ever read my book and validate my work. I thank Tim and Jan Greene for their encouragement throughout the process.

Finally, I would like to thank the community at my school for their support following my mom's sudden passing from Breast Cancer on October 30, 2017. Specifically, I am grateful for Hopkinton High School staff members Kiely Murray, Kirsten Gleason, Sarah Patterson, Valerie von Rosenvinge, Michael Webb, Lisa Winner, and Shari Meyer. These wonderful people have made my time in high school truly special.